MAGGIE CASPER
LENA MATTHEWS

MAVERICK'S
Black Cat

ELLORA'S CAVE
ROMANTICA PUBLISHING

An Ellora's Cave Romantica Publication

www.ellorascave.com

Maverick's Black Cat

ISBN # 1419954164
ALL RIGHTS RESERVED.
Maverick's Black Cat Copyright© 2005 Maggie Casper & Lena
Matthews
Edited by Mary Moran
Cover art by Syneca

Electronic book Publication September 2005
Trade Paperback Publication March 2006

Warning:

The following material contains graphic sexual content meant for mature readers. *Maverick's Black Cat* has been rated E-rotic by a minimum of three independent reviewers.

Ellora's Cave Publishing offers three levels of Romantica™ reading entertainment: S (S-ensuous), E (E-rotic), and X (X-treme).

S-*ensuous* love scenes are explicit and leave nothing to the imagination.

E-*rotic* love scenes are explicit, leave nothing to the imagination, and are high in volume per the overall word count. In addition, some E-rated titles might contain fantasy material that some readers find objectionable, such as bondage, submission, same sex encounters, forced seductions, and so forth. E-rated titles are the most graphic titles we carry; it is common, for instance, for an author to use words such as "fucking", "cock", "pussy", and such within their work of literature.

X-*treme* titles differ from E-rated titles only in plot premise and storyline execution. Unlike E-rated titles, stories designated with the letter X tend to contain controversial subject matter not for the faint of heart.

About the Authors

❧

Lena Matthews spends her days dreaming about handsome heroes and her nights with her own personal hero. Married to her college sweetheart, she is the proud mother of an extremely smart toddler, three evil dogs, and a mess of ants that she can't seem to get rid of.

When not writing, she can be found reading, watching movies, lifting up the cushions on the couch to look for batteries for the remote control and plotting different ways to bring Buffy back on the air.

❧

Maggie Casper's life could be called many things but boring isn't one of them. If asked, Maggie would tell you that blessed would more aptly describe her everyday existence.

Marrying young and being loved by a great husband and four gorgeous daughters should be enough to make anybody feel blessed. Add to that a bit of challenge, a lot of fun and an undeniably close circle of friends and family and you'd be walking in her shoes.

Speaking of challenges and fun, when not writing, Maggie's alter ego spends her time fighting fires and treating patients as a Lieutenant and Advanced Emergency Medical Technician with the local fire department. These awesome people are like her second family, no picking and choosing, they're just stuck with her.

A love of reading was passed on by Maggie's mother at a very early age, and so began her addiction to romance novels.

Maggie admits to writing some in high school but when life got in the way, she put her pen and paper up. Seems that things changed over the years because when she finally decided it was time to put her story ideas on paper, the pen was out and the computer was in. Took her a while to catch up but she finally made it.

When not writing, Maggie can usually be found reading, doing genealogy research or watching NASCAR.

Maggie and Lena welcome mail from readers. You can write to them c/o Ellora's Cave Publishing at 1056 Home Avenue, Akron OH 44310-3502.

Also by Maggie Casper

ഇ

Christmas Cash
O'Malley Wild: Hayden's Hellion
O'Malley Wild: Honoring Sean
O'Malley Wild: Zane's Way
O'Malley Wild: Tying the Knot

Maverick's Black Cat

৶

Dedication

๛

*To our understanding husbands, who put up with long hours,
late phone calls and sex in the name of research.*

Love,

Maggie & Lena

Trademarks Acknowledgement

~

Chapter One

✋

Eww, eww gross! Catarena Vaughn thought as she read the instant message that popped onto her screen. This was the fifth message in less than two minutes and each had been worse than the previous. It was becoming increasingly obvious a girl just couldn't lurk on a cyber sex site in peace and quiet without being harassed.

BlackCat: No, I don't want to pretend to be your sister and cyber with you.

Catarena typed back, muttering "freak" to herself as she closed the box. Sitting back in her chair, she took her fingers away from the keyboard in disgust. This was so *not* going the way she had planned. It was astonishing the things people would do to get off in this day and age, and with a million people available at the click of a mouse, there was someone out there willing to act out even the most bazaar of fantasies.

As a writer, she found it completely amazing, but as a single girl in Los Angeles, she found it completely frightening. Catarena wondered just how many of these guys she had let buy her drinks in a nightclub thinking they might be the one, when in reality, they just wanted to tie her up and pee on her. It was a very scary thought.

Scrolling down with her mouse, she checked all the names listed on the side. It was almost easy to figure out everyone's fetish from the names they made up. There were a few daddies and naughty subs, even a few Masters, which she was the most interested in. Catarena had been playing around with the idea of writing a novel about BDSM, a subject which intrigued her, but also one she knew nothing about.

Fetish.com chat room boasted the most diverse clientele in California and Catarena had secretly hoped to exchange information with a female sub who she might be able to pump for information. The one thing she noticed was although the clientele was large, it was mainly made up of males. Trying to find a female in this crowd was beginning to look damn near impossible.

Catarena had IM'd a few ladies, and to her amusement three of them were actually men pretending to be women and the other was afraid to talk to her off-line. It was beginning to appear her good idea wasn't going to pan out after all. Catarena couldn't write a tame romance novel to save her life. There was just something about her writing style and inability to keep her characters politically correct that mainstream publishing houses frowned upon. She had always known she was a writer—it had just taken fifteen years and a binder full of rejection letters before she dared allow herself to try a different avenue.

The very first time Catarena had picked up an erotic novel, she had been hooked. The passion and the boldness of the story had intrigued her so much so that she'd completed a short story of her own. The feedback she had received so far was encouraging. Since she now knew she was leaning in the right direction, Catarena wanted to try her hand at writing a BDSM novel. The topic was one that intrigued her, but now that she knew there was an audience for what she wanted to write she was stumped. Who got writer's block before they even wrote a word? she wondered disheartened. It was enough to drive a saint to drink.

BigEnuff: Hey, pussycat. You want to have a good time?

"Good night," she grumbled, closing this newest box, refusing to reply. It said right there in bold letters that her log-on name was BlackCat, a name she had put together from her long black hair and the nickname she'd had since childhood. Only here would the cat connotation be taken the wrong way.

As quickly as she had closed the box, another one popped up.

Eightinches: What's your fantasy?

Enough was enough already. Slamming down her soda, Catarena pulled her keyboard to her.

BlackCat: I am not interested in spanking, being spanked, calling you daddy or momma *that means you Naughtynanna* golden showers—giving or receiving—or anything involving the exchanging of, receiving of or starring in any films.

"That ought to do it," Catarena muttered, entering her rant onto the screen of the main room. She just wanted to watch. Maybe get a few ideas or pointers for the erotic novel she planned to write, not engage in any freaky-deaky stuff.

Princess: You might be in the wrong place then.

"You think," she grumbled, burying her face in her hands.

The bright, glaring light from her computer was beginning to give Catarena a headache. She knew she shouldn't be working in a dimly lit room, but it was the way she liked to write, especially of late, when her writing had turned a bit more risqué. The muted light hid the blushes she frequently acquired from some of the sites she had been surfing.

Taking a break from the computer, Catarena stood and stretched her tense muscles. She took a few seconds to work out the kinks in her back and neck from sitting so long at her desk. And a long time it had been. Surfing the net for subs wasn't as easy as she had thought it would be. With a sigh, she gathered her waist-length hair into her hands, instantly cooling her nape. It felt wonderful.

The tiny apartment she shared with her best friend wasn't known for its air-conditioning system and it was a constant battle for the two of them to keep their rooms cool. Not that it should have been that hard, her bedroom was the size of a portapotty. There was barely enough room to fit her desk and her queen-size bed, but Catarena refused to be without either.

Silently motivating herself to continue with her search, Catarena sat back at her desk and gathered her resolve. She wasn't going to let a bunch of horny men—and women—scare her away. Scanning the other available rooms, Catarena left the main board and clicked into a different room.

There were only two other people in the room, and neither of them had IM'd her, so that had to be a good sign, she thought. There was very little conversation going on there, and Catarena began to wonder if she might have stumbled into a private room. When a chatter first logged into a room, it didn't show the conversation that had been going on before, so Catarena didn't know if she was barging in on something.

BlackCat: Am I interrupting?

Catarena questioned as the other person who was logged in the room clicked off. When no one replied right away, Catarena wondered if they had been involved in an IM conversation of their own. She knew people moved out of the main rooms when they wanted to have a private conversation with someone else, and thought this might be the case.

Maverick: No. Hiding out?

The ding signaling a reply made her look up from her notes. He must have seen her post on the main board. Looking over to the left, she studied his name. Maverick. It had a cheesy Eighties feel to it, but it seemed harmless. There was a pool ball next to his name, a tamer icon considering some of the other ones she had seen.

BlackCat: Kind of. What about you? Did I scare away your friend?

Maverick: No, I'm just reading while I wait for someone to show up. The main room was getting a bit crowded for me, but it's past the time we were supposed to meet. I'm beginning to think I might have been stood up.

BlackCat: Getting stood up on a jerk site has got to be bad for your self-esteem.

Catarena chuckled at her own comment, waiting for the reply. When nothing came, she instantly felt bad. Not everybody got her brand of humor.

BlackCat: That was a joke.

Maverick: I figured as much but, of course, now it has me thinking…

A pervert who thought—finally her kind of guy. Smiling, Catarena took the scrunchie from around her wrist and pulled her long, dark hair into a bun, encasing it within the holder. Bringing her hands back to the keyboard, Catarena typed.

BlackCat: Sorry.

Maverick: Don't be. Well, I know why I'm here. What's your excuse? I think you alienated everyone here who might have wanted to chat with you.

Saw that, did he? she thought with a smile, tapping her pinky on the caps key.

BlackCat: That was the plan. I don't want to chat.

Maverick: Then why are you here?

Why did everyone keep asking her the same thing? she wondered, annoyed. Was it such a novelty to just want to lurk?

BlackCat: I just wanted to peek in and see what everyone was doing.

Maverick: Ah, a voyeur.

BlackCat: No. I'm merely curious.

Well, not really. Catarena just wanted to get a visual, a hands-on idea of what really went on. It wasn't as if she was going to masturbate to the happenings in the main room.

Maverick: About?

BlackCat: This seems like a roundabout way of you trying to get me to cyber.

Maverick: You came in my room, Kitten, not the other way around. If you want to go, don't let me stop you.

Regret filled her stomach as she realized Maverick was right. Catarena was the one who had gone in there and initiated the conversation. He had been nothing but polite.

BlackCat: No, I'm sorry, you're right. I guess I'm a little jumpy.

Maverick: Can't imagine why. This doesn't seem as if it's your kind of scene.

BlackCat: It's not, I'm trying to do research.

Maverick: For?

BlackCat: Don't laugh.

Maverick: How would you know if I did?

BlackCat: Good point, LOL, I'm trying to write a book. An erotica with BDSM in it.

Catarena could feel her cheeks heat in embarrassment. If she couldn't even type the word without blushing, how was she ever going to be able to write about it?

Maverick: And...

BlackCat: And I know absolutely nothing about the subject.

Maverick: Why do you want to do a book about something you obviously have such disdain for?

Startled, Catarena sat back and stared at the blinking cursor. Is that how it seemed? she wondered, reading over his reply again.

BlackCat: I don't.

Maverick: You don't want to be spanked or to spank.

Maverick copied her verbatim, typing back her own words to her.

BlackCat: You have to admit spanking seems a bit odd.

Maverick: Passing judgment on something you've never tried.

Catarena could hear the sarcasm dripping off the sentence almost as if he were in the same room as she.

BlackCat: What makes you think I've never been spanked?

Maverick: LOL. Kitten, I think it's a bit obvious.

BlackCat: You're making an assumption.

A correct one, she thought, grinning slightly, but that was beside the point.

Maverick: Well have you?

BlackCat: No, but still...

Maverick: LOL

BlackCat: What's erotic about hurting someone?

This was exactly the kind of information she had been looking for. Maverick was right—she would never be able to write about something she didn't understand.

Maverick: A spanking isn't about hurting someone. Sometimes it's about dishing out a punishment, sometimes it's about foreplay but it's never meant to hurt anyone.

BlackCat: Something tells me you've done it a time or two.

Maverick: A time or two, yes.

That's it, Catarena thought, staring at his words. Is that all he's going to say? Folding her legs up underneath her, she tried to get as comfortable as possible. She didn't want to miss a minute of this.

BlackCat: Are you a Master?

Maverick: No.

BlackCat: Are you a sub?

Maverick: Do I seem submissive to you?

Catarena didn't know the word for it, but he was so apparently not a sub.

BlackCat: No. Do you like to spank?

Maverick: I think spankings can be highly arousing. For the giver and the receiver.

Just reading his words caused her body to tingle. Never before had mere words affected her quite this way. Squirming a bit, Catarena couldn't help but ask more.

BlackCat: But you don't call yourself a Master.

Maverick: No. It's not a game I play, unlike some of these people. I am what I am.

What the hell did he mean? Catarena wondered, waiting for him to reply. Clicking on his name, she brought up his biography. It was empty. Just his name and the year he was born, which was a requirement to prove a subscriber was over the age of twenty-one. Although anyone with a calculator or half a brain could make one up.

BlackCat: What are you?

Maverick: Just a man.

Tapping her fingers on the desk, Catarena frowned. He wasn't being much help on the subject.

BlackCat: Then why are you here?

Maverick: I told you, an acquaintance asked me to meet them here. It's their fantasy, not mine.

BlackCat: Well, what's your fantasy?

Maverick: This seems an awful lot like cybering to me.

Catarena rolled her eyes at the screen. Rat bastard was throwing her own words back at her.

BlackCat: I'm just curious.

Maverick: So am I.

BlackCat: What are you curious about?

Maverick: You.

He released a breath of annoyance. Evidently, she wasn't the sassy-mouthed woman he'd thought her to be. It was probably better if she didn't answer him because Mason had a tendency to gobble up meek little girls whole.

At first, it was fine, but lately he hadn't been hungry for the simpering Barbie-doll types. These days his tastes ran more toward a strong woman, one he could tame. One who wouldn't roll over and coo just because he'd commanded her to.

With a disgruntled shake of his head, Mason maneuvered his mouse until the blinking cursor was centered on the exit button. He'd had just about enough of the Internet and cybering for one night.

BlackCat: What is it about me that makes you curious?

The words flashed across his monitor screen, making him smile. His Kitten was back. Mason rubbed his hands together, the thought of her purring contentedly after a wild tumble made his cock twitch. The thought that this unknown woman with her quick retorts and inquisitive mind could actually turn him on was disconcerting.

Mason was intrigued and that was saying a lot. The thirty-six-year-old was jaded to say the least. He had a tendency to accumulate women the way most boys accumulated baseball cards and had no qualms about setting the most ruthless of the gold diggers off with nothing more than a bauble or two for their time and the use of their luscious bodies.

If he didn't love women so much—their taste, the sound of their breathless moans as he played with their helplessly aroused bodies—he would have given up on the fairer sex long ago in exchange for a life of celibacy.

Mason, using the screen name "Maverick", had agreed to meet his latest piece of fluff in the Fetish.com chat room. But he'd grown bored very early at all the people chatting about the *lifestyle*. Hell, either you are dominant or you aren't, he thought to himself. For the life of him, Mason couldn't figure out the whole lifestyle thing. He didn't understand how someone could just choose to be dominant. And then *she'd* popped in, a smart-ass comeback for every perverted come-on thrown her way.

Maverick: I just think it's a bit strange you showing up at a BDSM community for research and yet you ask no questions or make yourself available in any way.

BlackCat: I've never been to one of these places, so excuuuse me for being a little unnerved about some of the things I've come across. Some of these people are way beyond freaky.

It was almost as if he could hear the sarcasm drip from the words flashing before his eyes. He'd bet a million dollars she was huffing in indignation. With an attitude such as hers, she'd forever have a sore ass if she were to be paired with a man like him. The palm of his hand tingled at the thought.

Maverick: Don't get sassy with me, Kitten.

BlackCat: Oh, pul-leez. I thought you said you weren't a Master?

Mason's breath whooshed from his lungs as he scooted his chair away from his desk. His eyes searched the dark interior of the room, allowing himself time to calm down. The woman was a complete stranger on a computer and yet she had the power to aggravate him. He thrust a hand through his hair then scooted his chair back into position to type.

Maverick: I'm not, at least not in the way you're thinking. You said you were researching a book—a BDSM book?

Mason had once chosen the lifestyle, even going so far as owning slaves and showing them off because it was what was expected. He'd been young and confused—naïve. He hadn't understood it then and he didn't understand it now. Being dominant wasn't a lifestyle *choice* for Mason—it was his life. It was as deeply integrated into him as was his heritage.

Figuring it out had been a hard lesson full of disappointment in both himself and the company he'd kept while living the lifestyle in various clubs and groups. Coming to grips with who he was had been like opening the door on a whole new world.

Mason might not live the BDSM lifestyle anymore, but he knew plenty about being in control. Maybe the name on the screen, the woman he'd already begun to think of as "his Kitten", would be willing to have a bit of a cyber relationship with him.

She'd get a research partner and he'd get... Mason wasn't quite sure what he'd get out of it, but whatever it was, it would be a hell of a lot cheaper than some of the arm candy he'd been dangling lately.

BlackCat: Yeah. But after visiting this place, I'm not so sure.

Mason couldn't help but chuckle as his fingers flew across the keyboard. Just thinking about a possible relationship, even an online one, was enough to make him hard.

Maverick: I'll make a deal with you.

BlackCat: What kind of a deal?

Maverick: The kind of deal where you get all the research material you could possibly need…and I get the control I always insist upon.

Once again his cursor blinked. The lack of a quick answer could mean several things. Mason didn't want to think about any of them, he wanted his Kitten to answer and, eventually, to submit.

BlackCat: Tell me more.

Maverick: Do you have an instant messaging program installed on your computer?

Instead of delving further into what was on his mind, Mason decided to stick with an easy question. For now anyway.

BlackCat: Yes. Why?

Maverick: Meet me for sessions. The first ten minutes are yours to ask questions. After, I'm in charge and you'll do as I say.

BlackCat: If you aren't a Master and you don't normally come to this type of place, then what exactly would I be learning from you?

Mason rolled his shoulders, an effort to loosen the tension building there as his fingers flew across the keyboard. At least his Kitten was intelligent enough to ask questions before jumping in feet first.

Maverick: I may no longer live the BDSM lifestyle but I know plenty about being in charge. Is it a deal or not?

Mason was ready to get on with it. He'd never had cyber sex or even phone sex for that matter — why do it when he could have the real thing with the snap of a finger — but there was just something about this woman. She made him want to keep her hanging on.

BlackCat: How often and why do I only get ten minutes?

Maverick: As often as I say and because the rest of the time you'll spend gathering information in a more hands-on sort of manner. Yes or no?

One, two, three, his cursor blinked before the single word flashed before his eyes.

BlackCat: Yes.

Mason gave BlackCat instructions for their first session then logged off and shut down his computer. It was late, the dark interior of the building quiet. After gathering his coat, Mason strode around his desk. He made his way through the dark interior and past the oversized leather couch dominating one wall, idly wondering what it would be like to take his Kitten there.

Mason shook his head to clear it of such lecherous thoughts then grimaced at the heat his body couldn't seem to shake. He continued his way out of his office and through the outer corridor then past the desk where his secretary normally sat. His mind whirled with ideas. He wanted Maverick's first private cyber meeting with his Kitten to be utterly unforgettable.

With the windows rolled down and the radio up just enough to be heard over the air stealing through the interior of his car, Mason headed his low-slung sports car home. For the most part, the trip was a relaxing one. It would have been completely relaxing if he could just get her out of his mind. Not that anything of the sort was likely to happen anytime soon, if the bulge beneath the fly of his tailored trousers was any indication.

Once home, Mason peeled the clothes from his body. Although impeccably tailored, his trousers had been uncomfortably confining throughout his cyber conversation. Completely nude, he picked up the pile of clothes. He silently moved across the plushly carpeted floor of his bedroom to the hamper where he eagerly disposed of the clothes.

Grateful to be rid of them, Mason strode to the bathroom where he turned on the shower then with a sigh of relief, climbed into the spray of steaming hot water.

After drying off with an oversized bath towel, he rifled through the top drawer of his dresser. Donning boxer briefs, Mason then poured himself a whiskey. The amber liquid sparkled against the glass and gave just the right bite on the way down.

A short trek to the den was made in bare feet with only the snug boxer briefs for cover leaving his flesh just chilled enough to keep the fire of arousal he'd felt earlier doused to a more tolerable level.

He made his way to the overstuffed leather sofa taking up one whole wall of his den. Before lowering his body to the cool, smooth surface, Mason grabbed the remote control. With the touch of a finger, music filled the room. The jazzy, sexy sound throbbed with a beat perfect for making love.

Mason sat his now empty glass on the end table, leaned his head back against the smooth leather surface then let out a deep breath as an effort to release the pent-up sexual tension he'd been holding onto since the unusual cyber conversation he'd been part of earlier. It didn't work.

If anything, he was even more aroused now than before. He couldn't picture her in the way he would a woman he'd seen before, but he could picture himself holding a woman closely. A woman unlike the emaciated, silicone-filled women who normally hung on his every move.

No, this woman was different. In his mind, their bodies swayed enticingly to the beat of the music. Without so much as a breath between them, her breasts would be pressed tightly to him, his thigh riding high between her legs wrenching a breathy moan from her full lips as he inflamed her body—mastered her arousal—with nothing more than the brush of his thigh against the heat of her sex.

The erotic thoughts running through his mind proved to be too much. In a flash, Mason had his cock free, stroking its length. He ran a finger over the sensitive head, gathering the moisture found there before he resumed the slow, languid pace keeping him on edge. He wasn't yet done fantasizing about his Kitten.

In his fantasy, it wouldn't take long until she was feverishly aroused. By then, he'd be more than ready to feel the warmth of her mouth closed tightly around him.

"I want your mouth," he'd whisper in her ear, nibbling its lobe until she shivered in his arms.

"I want to feel it wrapped tightly around my cock." Being the gentleman he was, Mason would help her to her knees.

He squeezed his shaft a bit tighter, enjoying the silky heat he felt there then gathered speed as he pictured her hands working his pants loose. He could almost feel as her fingers circled his shaft, they would be warm and gentle, unsure of how to continue.

Not one to spend too much time fantasizing—at least not since puberty—Mason was surprised at the clarity of the scene playing in his mind. Her hair was dark but he couldn't quite tell what color, and it felt like silk wrapped around his hand as he guided her mouth to his waiting length.

When her mouth settled around him, engulfing his cock head in moist heat, Mason struggled for control. He could see the scene play as if he were watching a movie behind his closed eyelids.

One hand was wound tightly in the length of her hair while the fingers from his other hand stroked her face. His thumb brushed her cheek as it hollowed with her increasing movements. He was getting close. The telltale tingling at the base of his cock warned him. The way his balls drew up close to his body gave clear indication.

"I'm going to come, Kitten." There was no urgency to his words, only pure ecstasy as she moaned low in her throat, sending a shockwave of sensation through his shaft.

"All of it, baby. I want you to take everything I give."

In his mind, his hand tightened in her hair as he held her head still, fucking in and out of her mouth. He loved the way her tongue played him, her lusty moans growing as her hand fondled him from below.

In actuality, something snapped, causing Mason to lunge for the small towel he'd thrown over the arm of the couch after his morning workout. His hand continued to pump as he came into the towel.

When he regained use of his body and brain, Mason lifted himself from his seated position. His legs felt weak, his body spent. Clutching the soiled towel in his hand, Mason left the room.

"Holy hell," he mumbled as he headed through the den and down the long hallway to his bedroom. Mason slipped between the cool sheets of his bed, physically sated yet emotionally ready for the first scratching and clawing go-round with his sassy-mouthed Kitten.

Chapter Two

ත

It was official, Catarena was finally as freaky as everyone she had ever met online. She couldn't get Maverick or the possibility of tonight out of her head. All day long, as she strolled the halls of her job, she wondered what he was doing. Was he a nice, single, normal guy—or was he a creepy guy whacking off in his basement while his kids and wife waited upstairs? It was a very unappealing thought, but a realistic one, nevertheless. Yet, there she was pacing back and forth in her bedroom while she waited for him to sign on.

"This is crazy," Catarena said to herself as she stopped in her tracks, glancing over at her computer debating for the fiftieth time if she really wanted to meet Maverick for an Instant Message rendezvous.

Would he ask her to do something she was uncomfortable with? Would she do it? It was the main thing she could see that appealed to people, the mystery of the unknown. There was no way the person on the other end could really know if she was doing what she'd been told to do, so she still didn't understand how people could get into it. In all reality, it would be hard to masturbate and type. She wasn't going to try it, of course, or at least she didn't plan on it. Hell, maybe she was too practical for this kind of thing, which would really suck because she really wanted to try and understand it.

Catarena glanced at the clock as she walked across her bedroom to close the door. There was no way in hell she wanted Bailey, her roommate, to walk in on her. Bailey wasn't the type to judge, but she would tease Catarena unmercifully. It's what Catarena would do in her place, if the situation was reversed, so she would expect nothing less of Bailey. They had been friends for way too long to let something as deviant as cyber sex slip away unnoticed. It was bad enough Bailey was already kidding her about her book, but if she got wind of this, it would never end.

The idea for her BDSM book wasn't something she had just pulled out of a hat of erotic ideas. It appealed to her on a basic level. The thought of giving up control to someone and putting her safety and sexual gratification in their hands was something she couldn't on a whole understand. Yet, it was something she had to admit engrossed her, and what better way to find out about it than to use herself as research.

Yeah, right, she thought with a chuckle, this was all about research. Research was the excuse she was giving for blowing off dinner with friends so she could rush home, shower and change for her cyber date. A cyber date, for Christ sake! She was a very attractive woman who was creaming over an encounter with a complete stranger who, for all she knew, played Dungeons and Dragons in his underwear every night.

For some reason, though, Catarena didn't see Maverick that way. He seemed different than the cyber nerds she had met in college. More intense, as if he didn't need to prove himself to her or anyone else, and it was exciting. Catarena closed her eyes as she sat down on her blue downy quilt, trying to imagine her phantom man in the same room with her, standing behind her and silently urging her on. Touching her lips with his smooth fingers, unbuttoning her shirt, moving down to—

The knocking of someone entering her buddy list drew Catarena from the erotic spell she had cast upon herself. Sitting up, she moved quickly over to the computer and hit the space bar, bringing the sleeping computer to life. Her newly added buddy was there, on time, as he had said he would be. She was still invisible, so she could easily close up and he'd never be the wiser.

It would probably be the smartest thing to do. The thing the good girl would do but, then again, the good girl wouldn't be writing an erotic novel in the first place. Catarena gathered what was left of her shaky nerves and clicked on his name, bringing up a private box. She nervously tapped her fingers lightly on the keyboard trying to think of a witty line.

BlackCat: Shall we play a game?

Catarena tapped her bare feet on the carpeted floor, waiting to see what his reply would be. Silence greeted her, making her wonder if maybe her joke was one of those things that was only funny when she said it to herself. Or maybe, she thought to herself, he just wasn't a Matthew Broderick fan. Tired of the silence, she posted again.

BlackCat: It was a joke. A reference to the movie *War Games.*

Maverick: I recalled the line, I was just wondering if you always joke when you're nervous.

BlackCat: What makes you think I'm nervous?

Maverick: Just a guess. Are you?

"You think," Catarena said aloud, but refrained from typing in her sarcastic comment, instead going with the other thought racing around in her head.

BlackCat: You have to admit this is a bit strange.

Maverick: I'm not going to bite.

There was a brief pause before another line popped up.

Maverick: Unless you want me to.

BlackCat: I thought you were the one in control.

Catarena typed with shaky fingers. It felt as if she were acting out some naughty-nymph girlhood fantasy.

Maverick: Part of being in control is knowing what pleases your partner and acting accordingly. Would it please you for me to nibble on you?

"Would it ever," she muttered, before she could stop herself. Catarena needed to backpedal and fast. If she wasn't careful, Maverick was going to gain control of the situation.

BlackCat: I thought I was the one who was supposed to be asking questions.

Maverick: I thought you were trying to work up the nerve to ask a question, but just so you know, your ten minutes started the minute you typed your first message to me.

Damn, he was bossy, she thought with a smile. Picking up her notebook, she looked down at her scribbles, trying to decide what her first question should be. She had made a list several pages long, but now they all seemed so unimportant. Putting the notepad back down, she stared at the screen for a second and decided to go with her gut.

BlackCat: What does BDSM mean to you?

Maverick: It doesn't mean anything to me. It's a catchall phrase, Kitten, with many different layers and levels. You might spank or enjoy being spanked, or even experiment every now and then with tying your partner up, but that doesn't necessarily mean you're into BDSM. It's hard to explain and even harder for most to understand. For me, it isn't a matter of conforming to a specific discipline, it's just who I am, a man who insists on control, about dominating someone completely. It's about what I like in my personal life and sex play to the mutual satisfaction of my partner. To be truthful, I don't understand it. I don't see how someone can choose to be dominant or not. Either you are or you're not. It's not a lifestyle choice.

BlackCat: If you don't understand it and you don't live the lifestyle, how do you think you can help me?

Maverick: I might not be living the lifestyle per se, but I know about needing to be in control.

Catarena paused and stared at his words. Maverick had done it again. He had used the word control. Catarena glanced over her shoulder to her queen-size bed. The adult magazine lying on its neatly made surface stood out like a sore thumb against the blue downy quilt. The cover of the magazine had caught her attention so she'd bought it—for the sole purpose of research. Or at least that was what she kept telling herself.

A woman bound with metal cuffs was prominently displayed. Her first glimpse of the cover had immediately brought Maverick to mind and now that he'd brought up the subject, she couldn't help but to ask.

BlackCat: What do you mean when you say control? Do you want to own someone? Is it a possessive thing for you?

Maverick: Full of questions aren't you, Kitten?

BlackCat: I only have ten minutes. I'm trying to use every single second to the max.

Maverick: There's always tomorrow.

Not if I can get it all done tonight, she thought, looking at the screen. Part of her wanted to extend the experience and milk it for all it was worth, but a smaller part—the Chicken Little complex—was holding her back.

Maverick: I think you're confused by the whole giving up control issue. The person who dominates is not always the one in control, Kitten. It's an ultimate power trip, but it's a mind trip, nevertheless. That's why, for me, it's not a game. It's not something I can log on and pull out of a closet. It's who I am twenty-four/seven. In my work, in my home, in me.

There was something about what he said—the way he said it—that made her want to squirm in her chair.

BlackCat: So the power is knowing it's not a game.

Maverick: NO. The real power is knowing the person who you have before you wants—no, needs—to please you.

BlackCat: Why do you want that?

Maverick: Why do you want to give it up?

BlackCat: This isn't about me.

Sitting back, Catarena's eyes widened in shock. This was getting out of hand quick. There was no way she was going to admit to him something she was having a hard enough time admitting to herself. Catarena hated the fact Maverick was reading her so well.

BlackCat: So basically this is about you being a control freak.

Maverick: I wouldn't say "freak", but I definitely want to have my way.

There was a real surprise, she thought with a smile.

BlackCat: Did you have a disturbed childhood?

Maverick: LOL, far from it. Are you trying to justify my desires?

BlackCat: Can they be justified?

Maverick: To myself or to you?

Catarena grimaced. Maybe she was coming off a tad condescending.

BlackCat: I'm trying not to be judgmental.

Maverick: You don't have to worry about offending me, Kitten. I'm a big boy.

BlackCat: How big?

Oh, God! Catarena brought her hands to her mouth in shock. She couldn't believe what she had just typed. *Where was the back button when you needed it?*

BlackCat: Let's pretend I didn't ask that.

Maverick: Why don't you just ask me not to breathe, it would be easier?

BlackCat: You're making this hard on me.

Maverick: I assure you, Kitten, you're doing the same for me.

Catarena could feel the heat rising in her cheeks, but it wasn't the only thing getting warmer. Her entire body felt as if it were on fire. The cool room was becoming warmer, and her body taut. Looking at his sentence longer, she reached down and slowly typed the words she was dying to know.

BlackCat: Literally or figuratively?

Maverick: What do you think?

BlackCat: I'll tell you what I think—I think you're spoiled. I bet you're an only child.

Maverick: And I bet you were thinking about this all day. You've probably been sitting in front of your computer for the last hour, trying to talk yourself out of meeting me here tonight.

It wasn't an hour, she frowned, looking over at the digital clock on her desk, more like thirty minutes.

BlackCat: I thought I was supposed to be asking the questions.

Maverick: Was I right?

BlackCat: No.

Maverick: Liar, but it doesn't matter 'cause your time is up.

BlackCat: Wait, I have one more question.

Maverick: Kitten...

BlackCat: Just one more.

Catarena had been avoiding this question the longest, mainly because she didn't know what to do if his answer was "yes". No, that wasn't true, Catarena knew what she would do.

Maverick: I'll give it to you, but you'll owe me a favor.

Raising an eyebrow at his words, Catarena smiled at the screen. The way he'd said it was intriguing, almost as if he were daring her.

BlackCat: Are you married?

The curser blinked for several seconds as Catarena held her breath, waiting for his answer.

Maverick: Of course not.

BlackCat: Why did it take you so long to answer?

Maverick: Because I was surprised you'd even have to ask.

Catarena let out a sigh of relief. It had been the most important question on her list. The one she had wanted answered more than anything.

BlackCat: Do you swear?

Maverick: Kitten, you're pushing it.

BlackCat: Please just answer me.

The cursor blinked for several seconds before he finally responded.

Maverick: I'm not that type of man, Kitten, as you'll soon see.

The woman was too much. Always ready with an answer, Mason was sure his Kitten was big-time trouble. A bundle of nervous energy. A woman on a research mission who had no idea she would be opening doors she might not be ready to handle, and because of it, he was going to proceed slowly.

BlackCat: So, do I just get naked right off?

Oh, hell! Mason thought, as the length of his cock tented the front of his gray sweatpants. Definitely trouble. He was going to prove to her he wasn't just some pervert getting off at his computer if it was the last thing he did.

Maverick: Not just yet, Kitten, keep your clothes on…for now. And watch your screen because I insist on promptness.

When no reply came, Mason decided to let her sweat it out for a minute. He'd give his Kitten some time to come to terms with the newness of their relationship. He leaned back in his chair then propped his feet up on the surface of the desk. When he thought she'd had long enough to do a little thinking, he pulled his cordless keyboard onto his lap and continued their conversation.

Maverick: First, I want you to tell me how you look.

An in-depth description of her was one of the things he wanted more than anything.

BlackCat: I have long black hair and blue eyes.

Her answer was straightforward, no-nonsense and boring as hell. Mason wanted to know it all, right down to what color and style of panties she was wearing.

Maverick: Tell me more.

BlackCat: More?

Mason tapped his fingers on the keyboard in irritation. It was mind-boggling how a woman he'd never before met in person could test his patience.

Maverick: Yes, Kitten, more. How long is your hair? What color of blue? How about your skin tone and your build? Paint me a picture with your words.

She was typing, the little box he was staring at on his computer screen told him as much, but it seemed to take forever. Mason wondered if he was making her nervous. He hoped so, at least a little bit. Just enough to keep her on edge.

BlackCat: My hair is my one big vanity. It is thick and black and curly, and when I wear it loose, it hangs to my waist.

Mason's breath quickened. He had a thing for hair, especially long hair.

Maverick: Very good, Kitten. Tell me more.

Tell me how it would pull across my thighs if you rode me through the night. Damn, how Mason wanted to say the words to her. Even more so, he wanted to feel her hair on him, see its glorious length fanned out across the pillows of his bed as he thrust deep into her body, but he couldn't say them. To do so might scare her away and then he would never find out the real of what he wanted to know.

BlackCat: My eyes are a deep blue, sometimes they even look black. I don't tan very well so I guess you could say my skin is pale, I've never really thought about it.

Mason nodded his head slowly as he read her words. He was getting a brief mental picture of how his mystery woman might look. Over and over, he came up with wet-dream material.

Maverick: Your body now, Kitten.

BlackCat: I'm five feet six but not skinny like the models you see nowadays.

Maverick: Size? Shape?

Mason typed the words quickly. He thought he might be going into caveman mode. He wanted more—needed to know every possible thing about her. He was absorbing every answer she gave, saving it all up for later so he could put it all together into a whole, wonderful mental picture.

BlackCat: Sheesh! Anything else?

Maverick: Size and shape, Kitten. Don't forget who is in control here.

He could almost picture her face scrunched up in irritation. Would her toe be tapping an impatient rhythm or did she have another little telling quirk?

BlackCat: Fine then! I'm a size ten and although not fat, I have more curves than most would consider fashionable. And just for the record, I like my body.

Mason smiled at her answer. He was damn glad she liked her body. Hell, he hadn't even seen it and he was already in lust.

Maverick: Glad to hear it, Kitten. A woman who enjoys her body is so much sexier than someone who spends all her time trying to hide it. Now, tell me what you have on.

BlackCat: I have a deep purple, flowing, ankle-length skirt and a white button-up blouse. My comfort clothes.

Maverick: Do you have a small mirror?

BlackCat: Umm, it's not small but it's not big. It's hanging in the hall.

Perfect, Mason thought, and hoped like hell he wouldn't scare her off. He stared across the wide expanse of his room to the huge mirror hanging on the far wall and wasn't so sure he'd be able to follow through if their roles were reversed.

Maverick: If you can, go get it. Let me know when you get back.

Mason took the time to pour himself a drink. Several minutes passed before she let him know she'd done as he'd asked.

BlackCat: I'm back. What do I do with the mirror?

Maverick: Set it up on your desk, next to your computer so you can see yourself.

It was coming down to the wire. Mason couldn't wait to see what her reaction would be.

BlackCat: Okay, I'm done.

Maverick: Good. Now I want you to unbutton your blouse. Watch yourself as you do it. When you're done, just let it hang open.

Nothing came across his screen. No denial, no acceptance…nothing. Mason waited as patiently as possible. It was hard, especially when he wanted nothing more than to insist she answer or, even worse, to find out who she was and go to her.

BlackCat: I'm doen. What now?

The typo was telling. He could picture her trying to type with her fingers trembling slightly.

Maverick: If your bra fastens in the front, open it. If it doesn't, pull it low until your breasts spill over the top of the cups.

BlackCat: I'm not wearing a bra.

Mason smiled when a little icon with blushing cheeks popped up next.

Maverick: Even better. Now tell me what color your nipples are.

BlackCat: They are a combination between brown and pink…I think.

Maverick: Do you have any toys?

Mason wanted her to run a vibrator over the twin peaks until they stood proud and erect. He could almost bet they'd change color then. He wanted his Kitten to see the changes in her body as it responded to erotic stimuli.

BlackCat: I don't own any. I've thought about it—I've just never bought any.

Maverick: No problem, Kitten. We'll take care of it right now. Keep your shirt open but grab a pen and paper. I want you to make a list. The first thing I want you to do is to set up a post office box where I can send you things. Set it up so I can send things to you as BlackCat.

Mason sent the message then waited briefly to see if she had any questions. When none came, he continued.

Maverick: I also want you to set up an anonymous email address. When you have it, send it to me here. Do you understand?

BlackCat: Yes.

Maverick: There is one last thing I want you to do before we log off for the night. You ready?

BlackCat: Yes.

Maverick: Lift your skirt until it rests in your lap. Are you wearing any panties?

Mason waited through several heartbeats, holding his breath for her answer.

BlackCat: It's lifted and, no, I don't have any panties on.

Mason's mouth watered thinking about her sitting there with her blouse hanging open, her breasts unfettered. To think of her skirt hiked to her waist and her pussy bare was almost too much. It was almost as if he were back in high school, jacking off at every opportunity.

Maverick: Tilt the mirror so you can see yourself. Spread your legs just a bit and tell me how you look, what you see.

Mason sent the message then thought of something else. Typing quickly, he added to his instructions.

Maverick: No touching, Kitten, just look and tell me what you see.

His shaft was rock-hard and there was an ever-growing wet spot on the front of his tented sweatpants. Mason was going to follow his own rules, though, even if it killed him. If she couldn't touch, neither would he. This time, at least.

BlackCat: This is so embarrassing. Are you sure I have to do this?

Maverick: Right now, baby, don't make me ask again.

If she had been in his presence, in his bedroom, he would have given her a nice stinging swat for questioning him. In that way, this cyber stuff wasn't all it was cracked up to be, Mason thought to himself, waiting for her answer to show on the screen of his computer.

BlackCat: Good God, you're bossy.

The words flashed before his eyes, and he couldn't help the chuckle that slipped from his lips. Mason would bet a week's pay she not only needed a keeper but also someone who could keep her mouth occupied when she got too sassy. He stared down at the rigid length of his cock and groaned at the thought.

BlackCat: I keep myself trimmed but not shaved. Other than that, I don't know what to say.

Maverick: Sure you do. Tell me what you see.

BlackCat: I can't do this. I don't know what you want, Maverick.

Mason decided not to push. Soon enough he'd have her bringing herself to mind-numbing orgasms at her own hands. He might be letting her have her way, but he wanted to be sure she understood there would be consequences any time she disobeyed him.

Maverick: Okay, Kitten. You're off the hook, but since I can't spank you for disobeying me, I'm going to cut your question time during our next session down to seven minutes.

BlackCat: That's not fair!

Maverick: Fair or not, that's the way it is. It's time to go, but before we do, I want your word you'll open an email account tonight and set up a post office box tomorrow. Do I have it?

BlackCat: Yes.

Maverick: Good girl. Send me the email address and I'll send you instructions for tomorrow. Good night, Kitten.

BlackCat: Wait!

Maverick: What is it, Kitten?

BlackCat: You know what I look like but I have no clue about you.

Mason ran a hand across his face in aggravation. His Kitten liked to push. Giving in too soon would send the wrong message, and yet, he wanted to please her.

Maverick: Is it that important to you?

BlackCat: Yes. If I don't know what you look like, how can I picture you in my dreams?

The damned woman knew exactly how to get to him. Just thinking about her all warm and cozy in bed, naked and dreaming about him made his cock throb.

Maverick: Very well, Kitten. I have brown hair and brown eyes.

BlackCat: And?

Maverick: I'm six-feet tall and I like to keep in shape.

BlackCat: More. Tell me more.

Mason couldn't help but chuckle, but he'd given in enough already. It was time to set his Kitten straight about who was in charge.

Maverick: No more tonight, Kitten. Time for bed.

Message sent, Mason logged off. They hadn't mention daily instructions so there was no telling what her reaction would be—he couldn't wait to find out. While waiting for her to set up an anonymous email account and send him the information, Mason had a repeat of last night.

He jacked off.

Chapter Three

 හ

"Okay, what's with the silly grin?" inquired Bailey, moseying up behind Catarena as she pushed her mail cart down the hall. "You look way too happy for someone who's at work."

"Can't a girl just be happy to be alive?" Catarena asked, stopping at her last office for the day. Walking inside the small space, she placed the mail on the desk, turned and ran right into the hand Bailey was holding up like a traffic sign. Rolling her eyes, Catarena pushed her friend's hand down and said, "What?"

"Hmm. If I didn't know better, I'd say you're getting laid. But since my room's down the hall from yours and I washed your sheets this weekend, I know differently."

Catarena couldn't help but laugh, Bailey was one in a million. They had known each other since high school and had been joined at the hip ever since. Ebony and ivory, or as they liked to put in more realistic terms—Mocha Frappe and Butt White. "I'm not getting laid—yet."

At the same time they both knocked on the wall, and muttered "knock on wood" before breaking out into laughter, a high school ritual they'd started when they had both been dateless, and after ten years of friendship, they had accumulated a lot of rituals. Their close friendship was one of the reasons why it was hard for Catarena to keep this secret from Bailey. She was really torn. Part of her wanted to confide in her friend, and the other part would rather die first than admit she had let a stranger tell her to lift up her skirt.

For now it was her little secret, and it was killing her to keep it.

"Come on, girl, I know something's up. And you know if you don't tell me, I'm just going to go stalker on you and case your ass until you do."

"Bay, if I'm lying, I'm dying," she said, crossing her heart. Hoping God was looking the other way. "Nothing's going on."

"Fine then, don't share." Bailey pouted, her full bottom lip sticking out in a sulk. "Just for being a brat, here." Thrusting a box at her, Bailey crossed her arms. "Satan, told me to give it to you. I *was* going to be the good friend and deliver it for you, but now I'm going to make you do it."

Catarena looked down at the box and groaned. Stan Douglas, the evil troll who they had the displeasure of working under was afraid of the head honcho, so anytime he had anything to be delivered to the boss, he always assigned it to either Catarena or Bailey. Stan wasn't fond of either girl, mainly because they wouldn't sleep with him, and did everything he could to make their lives a living hell. "I hate him," Catarena muttered, tossing the box in her cart.

"Well, he hates you right back."

"So what? Are you saying I should have gone out with him?" Catarena shuddered at the thought.

"No, but if you'd have been rude to him from the beginning like I had, we wouldn't be having this problem."

"Yeah, because he's all about the love with you, right?"

"He hates me, but he knows better than to say anything directly. I'm not afraid to fight a troll."

"I'm not going to complain. I'm not going to complain. I'm not going to complain," Catarena repeated over and over to herself as she headed toward the elevator. "I don't see why

I have to do his work and my work too. If I'm not back in fifteen minutes, send the troops."

"Aye, aye, sir." Bailey snapped into a rigid stance and saluted. "I'm proud of you, sir."

Chuckling, Catarena entered the elevator and made her way to the very back. Leaning against the cool, metal surface, she turned her head and looked at her reflection in the shinning surface. She had been doing a lot of looking since she and Maverick's IM conversation three days ago. She was trying to think of herself in picture form, so when he asked another question, she would be able to answer him in better detail.

The fact she was trying to please him was a tad disconcerting, but she found herself doing it anyway. He'd said he loved long hair, so she was taking extra care with hers. Normally at work she wore it twisted it up in a bun, but lately she had begun to wear it loose, taking extra time in the morning to brush it until it shined. It was silly she knew but, still, she took extra pride in it because she knew he would.

They hadn't met for the last few nights, but they had exchanged emails. Quick one-liners mainly, mostly from him instructing her to do something. Sometimes it was as foolish as painting her toenails red, or to wear black lace panties to work. His emails were always followed by one of her own, with a question Maverick answered promptly. She was getting her research and he was getting…well, Catarena wasn't too sure what Maverick was getting out of it, but he seemed pleased.

The email this morning had been the most risqué, at least for her. Maverick had told her not to wear panties to work and to wear a long skirt. To her amazement, she complied and had never felt sexier. At first, she was nervous. Even though it was foolish, her heart raced every time someone stood near her, and every time a man looked at her, she wondered if he knew. The thought of how all anyone had to do was raise her skirt and she would be exposed, kept her pulse racing and her thighs damp all day. She'd even had to retire to the bathroom several times to clean the dampness from between her thighs, but she was never allowed to relieve herself. It was one of the many orders she'd received in her email, along with a "PS" instructing her to go to her post office box after work, something she was looking forward to very much.

The elevator doors opened and revealed an office larger than her entire apartment. Catarena just looked around, amazed at how the company she worked for banked more than some small nations. Catarena had only been inside the inner office twice, and both times she'd had to keep her eyes from popping out of her head. The outer office wasn't shabby, either. Fabrics of bright royal blues draped the cushions and windows. The entire room was centered around a massive oak desk, which was guarded by Mrs. Garner, his secretary, also known as The Dragon Lady who seemed older than time.

"Can I help you?" she asked firmly, but Catarena knew what she really meant was "who are you and why should I care".

Down, Dragon, Catarena thought, reaching into her cart. "I have a package for…"

The inner door opened and out walked two men, both immaculately dressed and both devastatingly handsome. Bypassing the dragon, Catarena handed the box to her boss, Mr. Broderick. "Sir, this is for you."

He studied her, eyeing her long hair for a few seconds, before taking the package from her outstretched hands. Catarena couldn't help but return the favor. He was a handsome man who towered over her five-six frame nicely. Not too tall that she had to strain to look him in the eyes, but tall enough for her to rest her head on his shoulders. His lips curved a bit as if he were fighting back a smile and Catarena had to resist the urge to smile at him — she didn't want him to think she was flirting, she had enough on her plate with one aloof man, she didn't need another.

Despite his wealth, she wasn't intimidated, just impressed. He appeared awfully young to be running a Fortune 500 business, but what did she know. She would never see his type of wealth, not even if she played Monopoly. Catarena never lucked out and landed on Boardwalk.

"Was there anything else you needed?" he queried, seemingly amused at her frank study of him.

"A raise?" she quipped, groaning on the inside at her smart-alecky reply. *I really have to stop kidding all the time*, she thought when his companion smiled, and her boss merely raised a brow. "A joke, never mind."

Instead of nodding to acknowledge she had tried to make a joke, he merely raked her over with his eyes. It was a bit unnerving and Catarena thought she had never been so lavishly appraised in her life. Bringing his puzzled brown eyes back to her face, he smirked at her reply. "I'll check into it."

Catarena let out a breath she hadn't known she'd been holding and nervously moved her hair back over her shoulder. She didn't care if he was lying or not, he hadn't fired her, so it was good enough for her.

Catarena quickly pushed her cart to the elevator praying for it to open up and swallow her whole. Despite the tingling in the back of her neck, which normally signaled when someone was staring at her, she refused to look behind her, letting out a small sound of relief when the doors slid open. Strolling all the way to the rear, she didn't turn back around until the doors shut behind her. Catarena slumped against the wall, happy she didn't have to face him every day. She could already tell that Mr. Broderick was a dangerous man.

Bailey was waiting for Catarena on the ground floor with her purse in one hand and her coat in the other. "There's a beer in our fridge with my name written all over it," she said, grabbing the end of the cart and yanking it out of Catarena's hands. Pushing it to the side, she slid in beside her and pressed the "closed" door button.

"I have to clock out."

"Already done, Satan was hanging outside the women's restroom with a strange look on his face. He-Man is freaking me out." Bailey shivered, closing her eyes as she leaned against the elevator wall. "I just want to go home and rest my dogs. I'm pooped."

"I...uhh...I have a stop to make first."

Bailey turned toward her and slowly opened her eyes. "Where to?"

"Mail Boxes Etc.," Catarena murmured.

"Why are you going there?"

"I'm expecting a package in my post office box."

As soon as the elevator doors slid open, Catarena was out of there, unfortunately, she had nowhere to run seeing as she and Bailey commuted to work and lived together.

"Since when did you get a post office box?" Bailey asked with a knowing grin.

"Since I started receiving the *Watchtower*," remarked Catarena sarcastically. "Can't I have a few secrets from you?"

"No." Bailey laughed. "You can try, but I guarantee I'll find out."

"Bailey..."

"Catarena…" Bailey whined back in the same tone. "Just tell me what we're picking up and I'll let it go. For tonight anyway."

"I can't tell you."

"You'd better."

"I can't " pooring at her friend over the roof of the Civic " —because I don't know what it is."

Bailey's brown eyes widened, as did the smile on her face. "You slut."

"I am not," she said, getting into her car. *Not really, maybe after tonight though.*

"Yes, you are," Bailey replied, buckling in beside her. "And I want all the juicy details. Who is he, where did you meet him and does he have any hot friends?"

"Maverick, the Internet and I have no idea."

"The Internet. You mean like on one of those cheesy dating sites."

"No, more like the cheesy porn sites," Catarena admitted, and winced as Bailey gave a high-sounding scream.

"Shut up! No, don't shut up. Oh, my goodness, Lucy, you've got some 'splanin' to do."

* * * * *

It hadn't dawned on Mason until that afternoon his Kitten could be anybody. There he sat on his leather sofa, sipping whiskey, surrounded by comfort, not having the slightest clue as to who she was. She could be sitting in a one-room shack, her computer held together with duct tape and baling wire, and he'd be none the wiser. For the first time since meeting her in the Fetish.com chat room, Mason was actually disturbed by the fact.

For all he knew, she could be a man. Mason shuddered at the thought. No, she'd listed her attributes, most of them anyway, in detail. Mason cursed under his breath as he pulled his tall frame from the couch and headed to his home office. It was almost time to meet his Kitten for another session of questions and answers. Only things would be a bit different tonight, a bit hotter. Tonight Maverick would be pushing BlackCat farther and harder than she'd ventured before.

She logged on right on time. If nothing else, she was prompt, Mason would give her that.

Maverick: Hello, Kitten.

BlackCat: Hi. What is it about spanking that turns you on?

Mason hooted with laughter, the sound filling the quiet of the room. It was a good thing he was alone. Normally one to stay in complete control, Mason's exuberant outburst would have garnered many inquisitive looks.

The damned vixen was trying to beat him at his own game. Evidently, she was still miffed about having her question time cut back for not obeying.

Maverick: Hard question to answer, Kitten. For me, it depends on whether the spanking is an erotic one or one meted out for punishment.

BlackCat: Tell me about the erotic ones. I don't know whether I'm ready to hear about the other yet.

Maverick: It's all about bringing about a new type of sensation—one so keen, so sharp, my partner's body can't help but respond. To watch a woman strip for what is to come, to watch as her trembling fingers fumble with buttons and snaps.

Mason waited to see if she wanted to interject anything. When his screen remained blank, his cursor blinking, he closed his eyes and thought about what was so erotic about spanking. What turned him on the most? Then, when he had the picture clear in his mind, he opened his eyes and began to type.

Maverick: It's even more erotic if she follows orders well. To watch as she drapes herself facedown over my lap or situates herself in whatever position I desire. It's hotter than you could ever imagine. She may be hesitant, extremely aroused or a combination of both, but she does it anyway, waiting with bated breath for the first contact between my hand and the flesh of her ass.

Just talking about it was enough to make his palm tingle and, as whenever he had an Instant Message meeting with his Kitten, his cock was rock-hard.

Maverick: The best part, though, is to feel her grind her hips helplessly as the heat spreads across her flesh and arrows straight to her core. To know I can get her off with no more than a light touch is a huge turn-on. Seeing the flush of her skin caused by my own hand is almost enough to get me there too.

He was almost there, just writing about it. Without giving her time to add anything, he finished.

Maverick: And just when she thinks she can handle no more and her cries change from gentle moans to pleading gasps, I stop and take her hard and fast. That, Kitten, is what turns me on about an erotic spanking.

It took a bit before she answered. Mason fervently wished he could see her face during the passing time. Of course, if he could see her face, there was a very good chance he'd bend her over the foot of his bed and do exactly as he'd just explained.

BlackCat: Wow! Very intense.

Maverick: It was, wasn't it? So is the real thing. Are you turned on, Kitten?

He wanted to know if his explanation had made her wet. Was she fingering herself without his permission? It was driving him crazy not knowing. There was no way he could keep complete control without seeing her—knowing it, left a bad taste in his mouth. Mason already had an idea of something he could do to at least partially fix the problem, an idea he'd been mulling over. It was something he'd have to check into.

BlackCat: I'm the one asking questions, Mav, or did you forget?

Mason caught himself smiling. The woman had a mouth on her, that was for damned sure.

Maverick: Ask away, baby, but be forewarned, if we ever meet, you and your sassy mouth have got a spanking coming your way…and I'm not talking about the erotic kind.

It might not start off erotic, but it sure the hell would end up being so, Mason told himself, a devilish grin curving his mouth.

Maverick: You're running out of time, Kitten.

BlackCat: What's in the box?

Mason was a bit surprised at the change in conversation. He'd expected more sexual questions. Apparently, she was very curious.

Maverick: You didn't open it?"

BlackCat: You said not to.

Her answer surprised him a bit. She seemed so damned curious. Mason could only imagine how torturous it must have been for her to wait.

Maverick: Good girl. Your time is up anyway, so go ahead now and open it.

BlackCat: I'll open it right now, but you know, I really hate it when you tell me "good girl". I feel like I'm missing out on a petting session or something.

Mason's cock twitched at her choice of words. No more than a second could have passed before another message flickered across his screen.

BlackCat: That didn't come out quite right. Forget I said it.

Maverick: I don't think so. Have you opened my gift yet?

Mason couldn't wait to find out what her reaction would be. He'd sent her an assortment of things, things he wanted her to use, to experiment with. He'd chosen each specifically with his Kitten in mind. The catalog he'd ordered them from lay open next to his arm on the neat surface of his desk.

BlackCat: Oh. My. God! Are you serious? I don't even know what half of this stuff is.

Maverick: You will soon enough, baby. Consider it more research. How can you write erotica if you don't have toys?

Mason was sure he was going to shoot his computer before he and his Kitten were done. Seeing the damned cursor blink, blink, blink was way too fucking annoying.

BlackCat: What in the hell are pleasure balls?

Maverick: You insert them vaginally. They're slightly weighed to keep your pelvic floor muscles nice and strong but they've got an extra kick to keep you on edge.

Mason waited patiently for her next comment—he didn't have to wait long.

BlackCat: The blue waterproof one is nice. Batteries included even, I'm impressed.

A wide-grinning icon popped up beside her words.

Maverick: Brat!

BlackCat: Umm, Maverick?

BlackCat: Yes, Kitten?

Mason typed his answer knowing she must have found the last item he'd purchased with her in mind.

BlackCat: Tell me this isn't what I think it is. I know you didn't buy me a freakin' butt plug!

Oh, yeah, she'd found it all right. Mason smiled a wicked grin, anticipating what was to come. If he had learned anything at all about his Kitten, it was she hated being pushed. He would bet his last dollar she'd be losing more question time before their session was over.

He rubbed his hands together—they tingled with the need to feel her flesh. Mason leaned heavily against the leather back of his desk chair and took a deep, cleansing breath. It was getting harder and harder not to insist they meet. When his arousal was back to a bearable level, he resumed typing.

Maverick: It's exactly what you think, baby. I take it you have no experience with the darker side of sex?

Mason would love nothing more than to be the one to teach her. He could picture her on her knees on the dark sheets of his bed. With her shoulders to the mattress, her cheek pressed against the cool, crisp cotton beneath her, he would introduce his Kitten to the wonders of anal play. His cock throbbed in readiness, causing Mason to curse.

BlackCat: You're on crack if you think I'm going to be shoving anything up my ass just because you say so.

There her mouth went again. Mason thought the best way to go about her latest snit was to completely ignore it.

Maverick: What are you wearing tonight, Kitten?

BlackCat: What you told me to.

Maverick: Good girl.

Mason knew he was being a jerk but he couldn't seem to help himself.

Maverick: Is your mirror in place?

BlackCat: Yes.

Maverick: Take the silver choker and put it on, Kitten. Pretend it's my hand clasping it around the pale column of your neck.

BlackCat: A collar, you want me to put a collar on?

Mason couldn't help the smile that quirked the corner of his mouth

Maverick: It's a choker, Kitten. A symbol of my dominance over you, of the control you've agreed to give to me for now. I want you to wear it while you're researching, it'll help you remember who is in charge of you.

Mason waited for a smart-assed retort to pop up on his screen. He'd probably pushed a bit too far too fast, but the thought of his Kitten wearing his brand, even if only in the form of a silver choker was a huge turn-on. When no message showed, he continued.

Maverick: Take the blue vibrator from its packaging, Kitten. Let me know when you're done.

BlackCat: How would you even know if I did it?

"Damn," Mason mumbled to himself. "I must have ruffled her feathers good this time."

Maverick: Because you'll do as I say, Kitten, even if it's only for research.

Mason thrust his hand through the thick waves of his brown hair in frustration and wondered if he'd want to fuck her so bad if she didn't have a witty comeback for everything. Her quirky sense of humor and sassy mouth turned him on beyond belief.

Mason could picture her struggling with the theft-proof plastic package the glittery blue vibrator had more than likely been packaged in. After the way the butt plug he'd sent had thrown her, Mason wasn't so sure she'd be able to accomplish it.

BlackCat: Okay. Now what do you have planned to torture me?

Maverick: **Kitten.**

Mason bolded the word "Kitten", using it as a warning, although he doubted it would do any good. The woman didn't seem to take his warnings seriously.

BlackCat: Okay, okay.

Maverick: You need to wash it with some warm water and soap, and then put the batteries in. When you're done, let me know you're back. Then loosen the sash on your robe and let those luscious nipples of yours free.

BlackCat: How do you know my nipples are luscious?

Maverick: Because you've told me exactly how they look. Now do as I say, Kitten.

Mason didn't wait for a response. Instead, he left his office, heading quickly for the kitchen. He wanted to be completely sober and coherent for this, so instead of whiskey, he opted for a bottle of water. By the time he made it back to his small home office his heart was beating wildly in anticipation. He mentally chided himself for being so aroused. Hell, it wasn't as if he were going to actually get laid.

BlackCat: I'm back.

Maverick: I want you to tell me what color your nipples are.

BlackCat: Again?

Maverick: Kitten!

Mason twisted the top off his water bottle and took a long swig from it. She was absolutely exasperating and he was having more fun than he could remember having in more years than he cared to remember.

BlackCat: They are a combination of brown and pink. Just like I told you before.

Mason shook his head. If it was the last thing he did, he was going to teach the brat a lesson, even if he had to track her down and find her to do it. Although, if his plan worked out, Mason might not have to take things quite so far.

Maverick: Turn your new toy on and run it over your nipples until you can't stand it. No coming, Kitten. Do you understand me?

BlackCat: Yes.

It seemed as if hours had passed by. It took every ounce of his willpower not to send her a message insisting she tell him what she was doing, how the vibrations against her nipples made her feel.

BlackCat: Why won't you let me come?

Mason wanted her to come, he wanted her to come on his fingers, against his tongue and most of all he wanted her to come around the rigid length of his shaft. Oh, yeah, he wanted her to come. Just not yet.

Maverick: What color are your nipples now?

BlackCat: Pink. Bright pink.

Maverick: Now, Kitten, do you see what I meant about the erotic changes I can force from your body, even if by your own hand?

BlackCat: Yes.

Mason could imagine the breathless whisper of her voice. He pictured in his head how it would be if she were sprawled beneath him on his bed. The weight of his body pressing into hers as he sucked her nipples until they stood proud and erect just the way he imagined they were now.

Maverick: Point the mirror down, baby, and spread those sweet thighs. I want you to describe your beautiful pussy to me, and this time, you'll tell me.

Chapter Four

ഇ

Catarena couldn't believe it. She was doing everything he asked, and wanting to do things he hadn't yet requested. Maverick was turning into her biggest vice, all with just the click of a mouse.

She moved the mirror until it was stationed between her legs and lifted her left leg, placing it over the armrest of her black computer chair. Catarena wiggled a bit on the chair and tilted back with her right leg against the floor. It was a strain, but she managed to anchor her bottom until it rested on the edge of the seat, and for the first time in her life, she got a full view of her love center. Vaginas by nature would never win a beauty contest, she thought with a frown, but there was something so exciting, so sensual, about her body aroused and opening up to accept him.

Although Maverick wasn't there in person, he was definitely there in spirit, and her body wanted to quench its thirst on him.

Maverick: I'm waiting, Kitten. Don't have me ask you again.

Moving the cordless keyboard closer to her, Catarena typed a response as quick as she could. If he thought she was going to be speedy typer *plus* champion masturbator, he had another think coming.

BlackCat: This isn't so easy, Maverick.

Maverick: I never said it would be. There's never anything easy about sharing one's body for the first time with a lover.

Lover. She paused when she saw the word and a shocking thrill coursed throughout her body at the idea of being Maverick's lover. She had to remind herself that this wasn't real—she couldn't afford to become attached to him.

BlackCat: It's not the sharing part I'm having a hard time with. It's the describing.

Maverick: You're thinking too hard, Kitten.

Catarena frowned at his words. He was acting as if she were being difficult on purpose and, for once, she wasn't.

BlackCat: You're the one who wants the in-depth details.

Maverick: Don't think. Don't search. Just tell me **now**.

Maverick had bolded the word "now", much to Catarena's annoyance. If he were going to be pushy, she would push right back. Maverick wanted details, she would give them to him.

BlackCat: Fine, there's two lips, a clit and a small hole.

Maverick: How small of a hole? Is it large enough to take the vibrator in it without any lube?

Catarena stared at the blue penis in her hand doubtfully. She wasn't a virgin, but it had been awhile since her last encounter and the vibrator seemed a bit big.

BlackCat: I'm not sure.

Maverick: Well we're just going to have to make our own lube. I want you to keep your legs spread and slowly rub the head of the vibrator around your lips. Watch yourself the entire time. Watch yourself as if it were me in the reflection staring back at you.

Catarena's body trembled at the words. More than anything else, she wished Maverick was in the room with her. She wished he was giving her instructions in person instead of over the computer. Pushing back again with her toes, Catarena turned the vibrator on low then moved it down slowly to her pink flesh. Following his instructions—as if he were in the room—she experimented with it slowly—allowing her body to get used to the vibrations coming from the toy.

Maverick: For the rest of this, I'm going to make it easy. Just type "Y" for yes you understand or "N" for no if you don't understand. Do you understand?

Transferring the vibrator over to her other hand, Catarena hit the Y button and spun her chair so she was still in the view of the mirror, but closer to the keyboard at the same time. She was happy he'd thought of the single letter idea, because God only knew how she would have been able to type and pleasure herself at the same time.

Maverick: Good. I want you to touch the hood of your clit. Not the front of it, but the top of it. Keep the vibrations on slow, but tap it lightly, so you're barely leaving it on you. Do you understand?

BlackCat: Y

Maverick: Good girl. You're making me so proud when you comply.

Catarena read over his words in amusement. He was proud and she was wet. Wetter than she could ever remember being. Some of it was the toy and the heavy weight of the silver choker circling her neck, but a bigger part of it was him and, damn it, Maverick was probably aware of the effect he had on her.

Maverick: Now stop with the tapping and slowly move the vibrator from the hood to the front, and down to your opening. Are you wetter?

BlackCat: Y

Maverick: Feather the tip against your ass for me. I want you to get used to as many sensations as possible. Learn to love every inch of your body, Kitten.

The sensation was different from anything she had ever felt before. The light, teasing caress was mind-numbing, making her want to, for the first time ever, explore her nether hole. There were quite a few firsts going on tonight.

Maverick: Take the vibrator and slowly—key word here, Kitten, is slowly—slide it into your pussy for me. Be careful and don't rush it, I don't want you damaging yourself. Don't push it in all the way. Only halfway in and then take it almost all the way out. You're stretching yourself, allowing your body to naturally accustom itself to the new sensation.

There was nothing natural about it, Catarena thought as she forced herself to do as he instructed. She was so fucking hot right now. With just one hard thrust, she knew she would come. But she withheld, pleasuring herself slowly, allowing her body to adjust as it begged to be satisfied.

Maverick: You're awful quiet, Kitten, is everything going all right?

BlackCat: N

Maverick: What's wrong? Is it hurting you?

BlackCat: N

Maverick: Then what is it? Type out your answer.

Catarena continued to torture her hot cunt as she pecked the keyboard with one finger. This was crazy, completely out-of-the-mind kind of stuff, but she was getting off on it.

BlackCat: I want 2 cum.

The curser blinked for several seconds, several long seconds as she continued to do as he instructed before his reply flashed across the screen.

Maverick: I want you to come too, Kitten, but not yet. Not until you've learned more about yourself.

Snatching her hand off the vibrator, Catarena furiously typed in her reply. She was hurting, aching to finish, and he was teasing her.

BlackCat: I know myself, damn it. I know I need to come.

Maverick: Not yet, Kitten. You need to learn some restraint, or maybe you just need to be restrained.

Never, she thought, returning her hand to the abandoned toy. There was just no way in hell she would allow someone to restrain her but, then again, she had never thought she would be masturbating for a stranger online. It was all so very surreal. Catarena's body was begging for relief. She was pushing up on the chair, trying to take as much in as she could, but for the life of her, Catarena couldn't push more than half in. Not because her body wouldn't let her, but because Maverick wouldn't.

Maverick: I want you to speed up your rhythm and push it farther into you. Farther until just the base shows and pull it back out. Then do it again. Each time faster and deeper than before.

Catarena could feel her climax moving over her body like a warm tidal wave was threatening to cover her whole. Her nipples had never felt so tight. Her body had never felt so moist. She was on fire.

Maverick: Are you still watching yourself, Kitten? Watching the way your pussy is eating up the vibrator. I want you to memorize the sight, the smell, the beauty of it all. Now imagine it's me there instead of a vibrator.

Her control was hanging on by a very fine thread. No matter how fast she pushed it in or how hard she thrust up to meet it, it just wasn't enough. She needed more. She needed Maverick there. Catarena's hands quivered as she pecked at the keyboard.

BlackCat: I can't.

Maverick: Yes, you can, Kitten. You can because I say you can. I want you to take your nipple between your fingers and pluck at it. Squeeze it as you pleasure yourself with the toy. I want you to remember how I picked it out especially for you.

It's yours, like you're mine. Fuck yourself, Kitten, and come for me.

Catarena's body broke before her will did. Unable to fight the pleasure any longer, she bit her lip, drawing blood as she came hard against the vibrating toy pulsing in and out of her body. Her eyes were locked on the mirror the entire time and watched through half-closed eyes as her pussy clutched to the toy as if it were a lifeline, pulling it deeper into her body as the orgasm ravished her body and mind.

It was different than anything she'd ever experienced before. The power of his words and the vision spread before her was as erotic as any lover she'd ever had. She removed the still buzzing vibrator from between her aching legs and dropped it to the ground as she laid her head back on her chair.

Her legs shook from being held so long in an awkward position and her body ached in places it hadn't in years. Catarena felt as shaky as a newborn colt, unable to get her legs to move underneath her.

Catarena rolled her head toward the screen and stared at the blinking curser as if she were staring at her lover's face. Moving her lethargic hand to the screen, she ran her damp fingers over Maverick's name, leaving a damp smudge on her computer.

Maverick: Kitten?

BlackCat: Yes.

Maverick: How are you feeling?

Catarena rolled her eyes at the screen and smiled softly. How did he think she felt?

BlackCat: Tired. Sore.

She just wanted to turn off the computer and climb into bed. Moving her leg down from the arm of the chair, Catarena sat up and stretched her legs out in front of her. The tingling sensation in her feet reminded her she'd had her leg up for far too long. Catarena reached down and picked up the towel she'd brought into the room especially for this occasion and gently wiped the tender spot between her legs.

Maverick: Where is the toy?

His question startled her, forcing her to look around for it. Catarena grimaced when she spotted it on the floor and felt slightly bad for abandoning something that had granted her so much pleasure.

BlackCat: On the floor.

Maverick: That's no way to treat a lover.

BlackCat: The toy is the best kind of lover. He knows when to go away.

Catarena just wanted to bask for a minute, not take notes and talk about things. Why couldn't he just allow her to revel in her experience? Why did he still want more?

Maverick: Did you watch in the mirror?

Did she ever. Even now, she was glancing over at herself, startled to see the way she looked. Her breast had slight red marks from where she'd dug her nails in when she came. Battle wounds. How intriguing. But if Maverick was wanting her to describe it, he had another think coming. It was bad enough she had gone and enjoyed it—much more than she would ever admit—but he wouldn't rest until she was cut open for him to see.

BlackCat: What do you get out of this?

Maverick: You know what I get out of this, Kitten.

Catarena frowned at his words. His answer didn't tell her anything. There she was feeling open and raw, and he was sitting somewhere probably enjoying the fact he had just made her get off. It wasn't fair.

BlackCat: Your cocky attitude is really annoying at times.

Maverick: Why are so you upset? Is this how you get after every orgasm?

BlackCat: You know the best thing about meeting online is you'll never really know if I had an orgasm or not. I could have been faking.

Yeah, right, and the pyramids were built in a day. There wasn't an immediate reply, which made Catarena wondered if maybe she'd gone too far. The blank screen made her nervous, making her wonder what he was thinking, but before she could get worked up about it, the typing message resumed. Catarena couldn't believe how relieved she felt, until his words appeared onto the screen.

Maverick: It's better not to tempt me right now, Kitten.

BlackCat: Why?

Maverick: Because I'm not going to get pissed off and log off. I'm going to get pissed off and take you up on your challenge.

BlackCat: I have no idea what you mean.

Maverick: You will. Trust me, Kitten. You will.

* * * * *

Mason had spent the better part of the day in a foul mood. He wasn't used to not being in control of every situation that affected his life, especially his sex life—if their cyber relationship could be called a sex life.

Leaving his office, he'd just made it to his car when his cell phone rang.

"Hello," he answered.

"You going to work yourself into a stupor tonight or do you have time to have a drink with a friend." Mason smiled faintly, immediately recognizing the voice on the other end of the line.

"I'm free, Sebastian, leaving the office as we speak."

There was a moment of dead silence on the other end as if the phone had gone dead. Mason pulled it away from his ear to look at the face. Nope, still working, he thought to himself.

"What's her name?"

Mason ignored the question. "I've got an errand to run first. You want to come with me or do you want to meet somewhere?"

This time there was no delay before Sebastian answered. "I'll come with you. I'm sure this has got to be good if it got you out from behind your desk before ten o'clock at night."

"If you only knew," Mason mumbled to himself before answering. "I'll pick you up at your place in a few then."

Mason hung up his cell phone with a scowl on his face. As much as he wanted to meet up with Sebastian, he knew the damned fool was going to harass him until he spilled the beans. And then he would laugh himself sick. It would be worth it though, because Sebastian was his closest friend, the only person he could talk to about what was going on. Besides, if their positions were reversed, Mason would harass Sebastian just as relentlessly.

His car whipped in and out of traffic with ease. Mason kept the windows down, the radio up and tried not to think about BlackCat. It proved to be virtually impossible.

He tried concentrating on the road and on the pedestrians crossing the street. Anything to take his mind off the fact he was going fucking nuts not knowing where his Kitten was or who she was with. The need to control, even while he protected and loved, had been integrated into him since his youth. It was the way he'd been raised. It was who he was. And he couldn't stop it, not even for a cyber relationship.

Mason wasn't so sure BlackCat had understood or even cared about his need for control. Maybe she was just humoring him for research purposes. Maybe she wasn't actually following any of his orders. Not knowing was beginning to wear on him. So much for not thinking about it, he thought wryly.

Sebastian emerged from his house after Mason pulled up and honked. Walking to the car as if he didn't have a care in the world, Sebastian was as opposite of Mason as the day was from night. Carefree and laid-back, the man didn't have a staid bone in his body.

"So where we going?" Sebastian asked, as he slipped into the passenger seat of Mason's sports car.

"To the computer shop first and then to pop something into the mail. After, we'll go wherever you decide."

Mason knew Sebastian had a million questions rolling around in his head but he didn't offer any answers. There would be enough time for those later. Right now, he was a man on a mission and he wouldn't relent until he'd finished what he'd set out to do. Mason had chosen the business that took care of the computers for Broderick Incorporated to accomplish his task. He'd already placed the call. It was just a matter of stopping by to pick up the package.

He skillfully pulled into the overly crowded parking lot then proceeded to wedge his car into a spot too small for a bicycle much less a car—even a compact car.

"I'll be right back." Mason hopped out of his car with purpose then strode across the parking lot and through the double glass doors to enter the business.

Glancing down at his watch, Mason growled when he realized what time it was. He was running low on time and if he didn't get the package sent before the mail went out for the day, it wouldn't make it to her by tomorrow. The fact that they lived in the same city was a pleasant surprise that would make it all the more easier when he finally decided it was time they meet face to face.

"What's that?" Sebastian asked when Mason returned to the car.

"In the bag is a webcam."

"And the box?"

Mason threw him a disgruntled look before answering. "Another webcam."

A shout of laughter exploded from Sebastian catching him off guard. Mason swerved as a result, earning himself a one-fingered salute from the car next to him.

"You dog," Sebastian said between gasping breaths of laughter. "You're worth millions and yet for some off-the-wall reason you feel the need to get into cyber porn." His friend was wheezing now, his laughter growing louder by the minute.

"Would you shut the hell up already! And, no, I'm not into porn, at least not the cyber variety."

Sebastian made a snorting noise in disbelief. "Then why do you need two webcams? Explain that one to me, buddy, ol' friend of mine."

"Just shut up, Sebastian. Let me get this to the post office before the mail goes out for the day. Afterwards, I'll spill the whole story."

His annoying friend was sitting in his car, a wide grin across his face when Mason came out of the post office. "Where do you want to go?"

"Some place real close. I'm dying to hear this story."

"Fine," Mason grumbled. He figured the sooner he got the whole thing out in the open—sharing with his best friend—the sooner he would feel better.

He drove a few blocks before pulling into The Office, a local bar where many of the local business people populated to wind down after a long day of work. The two of them ordered their drinks then found a table next to the window. Mason wasn't planning to stay long, he had an email with instructions to send to his Kitten.

Mason had barely started his story before Sebastian was laughing so hard he was in tears.

"I don't know what in the hell is so funny."

Sebastian was trying to stifle his laughter if the pinched look on his face was any indication but, evidently, he wasn't trying hard enough. "Whoo," Sebastian let out the breath he'd been holding. "You have to be on the outside, Mason, to see the humor in this."

Mason arched a brow at his friend. "Care to explain?"

"Well, hell, Mason, it's obvious. What I don't understand is how in the hell you think you can have an online relationship and still be in control...and don't give me that look, you know damned well you go crazy if you're not the one in control. It's the only reason you're snarling at me right now."

"I'm in control, idiot, just the same as if I had her under me in bed."

"Tied to your bed more like it. Have you forgotten I've known you since college?"

Mason muttered a string of curses. He had a feeling his friend was right but he hoped to hell he wasn't. The webcam he'd just sent his Kitten would have to be enough. He'd at least be able to see her even if he couldn't feel or taste her.

Sebastian wasn't happy to leave things well enough alone, though. Nope, his irritating friend had to push. "I know I haven't forgotten. Hell, I don't think I'll ever forget the time I walked in on you and your little blonde girlfriend. You had her all trussed up, fucking—"

Mason cut his friend off before he could give the group at the next table more information than he wanted shared. "Don't even go there, buddy. You may be all laughs and parties when in a crowd, but I've got a few stories I could share about you just the same." Mason absently scratched his chin. "Like the time you had Mary Ann McCormick naked over the pool table spanking her with…" Mason let his words trail off, then asked, "What was it you were spanking her with?"

Finally, Sebastian sobered. Mason couldn't help but chuckle. "Got your attention, did I?" No answer.

This time when Sebastian spoke, he was serious. "You're going to have to insist on meeting this woman, Mason, and you know it. This whole thing won't have a chance in hell otherwise."

"It's all for her research. It's not as if I was on the Internet looking for a relationship. Don't worry about me, it's all for fun."

Mason wasn't sure he believed his own words and from the look on Sebastian's face, he didn't believe a word of it either. The two of them finished their drinks and left the bar. They rode back to Sebastian's place in companionable silence as if they were busy mulling over the conversation.

Mason dropped Sebastian off, agreeing to get together again soon and then he was off. He couldn't wait to get home and install his webcam.

When he finally arrived, he carried the small bag into the house and went straight to his office. Within a matter of moments, he had the hardware connected to his computer and the program to run the equipment downloading. It was easier than he had thought it would be. While the program was downloading, Mason said a silent prayer hoping his

Kitten had a computer compatible with the webcam he'd sent her.

Mason showered then dressed in nothing more than some loose-fitting silk boxers. He loved the way the soft fabric felt against his heated flesh. Just thinking about his mystery woman was enough to set him on fire.

Relaxed and ready, Mason cleared away the box and owner's manual belonging to the webcam and logged on to his computer to send his Kitten an email.

Good Evening, Kitten.

Tomorrow you should receive another package from me so be sure to check your box before heading home from work. There will be a note for you inside your gift and a list of instructions. Follow them and don't be late, baby.

Maverick

PS. I warned you not to push.

Mason hit the send button then left the office, moving slowly but surely down the hall to his bedroom. Tomorrow was going to be a long day.

Chapter Five

"Oooh, I'm calling your momma." Catarena jumped and turned around, hiding the camera behind her back, but it was way too late, Bailey had already seen it.

"What are you doing in here?"

Leaning against the doorway, Bailey crossed her arms. "I'm watching you get set up for what appears to be a part-time job. What's your new site called, middle-aged women gone bad?"

"I am not middle-aged, bite your tongue."

"But you are old enough to know better, Cat. What is going on, boo?"

Catarena sighed and dropped onto her bed bringing the camera around to her lap. "I received another gift from my cyber buddy." Okay, it was a stupid name for what Maverick was, but it sounded a hell of a lot better than cyber fuck buddy.

"Candy and jewelry are gifts. A webcam is a *Penthouse* letter waiting to happen."

"It's all in the name of research." Catarena tried but she didn't believe it either, so she seriously doubted Bailey would. Like Huck said, "You can't pray a lie".

Nodding her head, Bailey tried to keep a serious face, but she couldn't prevent the twinkle of amusement from entering her eyes. "Right, I can buy the research thing but I thought this book was on BDSM not voyeurism."

"I'm working on the sequel." Catarena smiled, hoping Bailey might let it slide.

No such luck. Bailey roared with laughter. "You don't have to lie to me, baby girl, who am I to judge. I slept with Ralph Johnson, remember? Just be careful. Make sure he's not some freaky-deaky psychopath looking for a kinky thrill."

"I can handle freaky-deaky," Catarena kidded. "Psychopath on the other hand is another story. Maverick is fine." Controlling and domineering, she thought, but not psychotic.

"All right, but if they make a Lifetime movie about your death, I want to be played by Halle Berry."

Catarena rolled her eyes and held her tongue as Bailey left the room. She didn't want to give her any reason for further comment. Catarena had enough doubts for the both of them as it was. The funny thing was, though, she didn't have to do anything she didn't want to. It wasn't as if Maverick were going to burst through the door and force her to turn the webcam on. She had a choice. Just as she'd had before. The only thing wrong with her free will was its urging for her to plug the camera in and go deeper. Catarena felt like Alice in Wonderland, as if she were falling down a deep, dark, rabbit hole. The only problem was, she was enjoying it.

Catarena closed the door firmly, making sure she locked it. There was no way she wanted Bailey to accidentally on purpose burst in at the wrong time. Going to her desk, she uploaded the disk to her computer and finished reading the back of the webcam box. Catarena had to admit she was seriously amused Maverick had bought her one. Amused but not surprised. What surprised her most was that the man lived in the same town she did, and after her last little parting shot, she *had* been expecting something, it was just too funny what the "something" had turned out to be.

Talk about controlling, he was trying to make sure he had his way in all things. But if Maverick thought she was just going to roll over and beg, he had another think coming.

Coming back into her room after her instructed bath, Catarena felt extremely relaxed and peaceful. The hot bath mixed with the candles had really done the trick. She secretly thought Maverick was trying to loosen her up before he pounced. Knowing him, anything was possible. His instructions were part common sense and part ludicrous. It wasn't as if he had asked her to do anything strange or ridiculous, but to Catarena it seemed as if he were trying to pamper her, by making her pamper herself.

The bath made sense because she had just come home from work and it did help sooth her tired body, but the candle instruction seemed a bit odd. Maverick had instructed her to light no fewer than five candles and place them sporadically around the room, and to play a soft, relaxing CD, preferably light jazz or classical. It had soothed her, but she had also had to put up with Bailey's walk-by, knocking on the door and giggling, which thankfully would no longer be an issue since she'd just left to go out on a date.

Her damp hair lay loose around her shoulders air-drying as Catarena applied a generous amount of pear-scented lotion on her cool skin. She gently massaged her calves as she spread the lotion into her legs, taking time to enjoy her own body. Catarena had shaven, another instruction from his Lord and Master, and her legs felt smooth and soft to her touch. It had been a long while since she had spent so much time on herself.

A lyrical ringing from her alarm clock set in advance alerted Catarena of the time. She stopped what she was doing to light the candles she had taken into her room, giving her bedroom a soft ambiance to fit the mood she was in.

The silk fabric of her robe trickled down her back as she dropped it to the floor. Her nipples hardened instantly as her damp hair caressingly brushed against them, sending shivers down Catarena's already aroused nude body. She closed her eyes and took in a deep breath before sitting down in her chair, mentally preparing herself for the unknown. Let the games begin, she thought to herself as she logged on. Maverick was already there.

BlackCat: It's chilly.

Or it would have been if she hadn't turned up the heat in preparation for this meeting.

Maverick: LOL. Hello to you too, Kitten. I take it you're following the instructions and are wearing my choker and nothing else but a smile.

BlackCat: And six-inch stilettos.

There was a pause, followed quickly by his response.

Maverick: I didn't instruct you to wear stilettos.

BlackCat: It was a joke.

Catarena really wished there was a rolling eyes icon she could blast him with. The man had absolutely no sense of humor and, of course, the one thing he would jump on was that she wasn't following his instructions. Figures.

Maverick: Ahhh, I think it will take me a lifetime to get used to your **brand** of humor.

Catarena smiled when she saw Maverick had bolded and underlined the word "brand".

BlackCat: Well, I have the first three chapters started, so you can thank your lucky stars you won't have to put up with me for a lifetime.

Maverick: You do, do you? Will you let me read it?

BlackCat: Do you want to?

Maverick: Of course, I'm your muse.

Yes, he was, she thought with a smile. Still Catarena wasn't so sure how comfortable she'd be letting him read her story. It was silly, she knew. Here she was sitting naked because he'd commanded her to do so, but she didn't have the balls to let him read what she'd written. Maybe Maverick wasn't the psychopath in this relationship after all.

BlackCat: We need to hurry, before I catch a chill and my minutes are up.

Maverick: I can think of lots of ways to warm you up.

I'm sure you can, Catarena smiled wide at the thought. There were many ways she could imagine him warming her up, but she wanted to know what he imagined instead.

BlackCat: Have you ever given up control sexually to a partner?

Maverick: No.

Catarena rolled her eyes at his reply. There was a big surprise…not.

BlackCat: Why not?

Maverick: To be honest, no one's ever asked. I guess I don't attract the type.

BlackCat: Would you if someone asked?

Maverick: If I was properly motivated, I guess I would. "Never say never", Kitten. It's my motto.

BlackCat: Really, 'cause mine is "Fuck me once, fuck you, fuck me twice, fuck me". It might lose something in the translation though.

Maverick: LOL, I'm sure it does. French isn't it?

"Oh, my God!" Catarena said aloud in surprise. She was going to have a heart attack. It appeared as if she were wrong about him not having a sense of humor after all.

BlackCat: Did you really just make a joke?

Maverick: It's been known to happen.

BlackCat: Really? When was the last time?

Maverick: 1993, I believe. I'd say I'm due for another.

Another one, good Lord, he was on a roll.

BlackCat: Are you British?

Maverick: No, why?

BlackCat: Because you have a dry sense of humor, and you seem kind of stuffy. Let me see your teeth.

Maverick: ROFLMAO. I assure you, my teeth are well-maintained, my blood isn't blue and I don't have a pansy-ass accent.

BlackCat: I think the British accents are sexy.

Maverick: Ha. It's a common myth. Trust me, all British men don't sound like Hugh Grant. Some are rather nasally and annoying.

He was speaking as if he had firsthand knowledge. How cool is that? Catarena thought. The closest she had been to "out of the country" was when she and Bailey had tried to sneak over to Tijuana to go drinking, but their car broke down right outside the border.

BlackCat: Have you been to England?

Maverick: Yes. Have you?

BlackCat: Does Perris, California count?

Maverick: No, and the fact Paris isn't even in England would account for half of the reason the answer is no.

Catarena made a mocking face at the computer screen. Where was the damn sarcastic icon when she needed it?

BlackCat: The answer would be no.

Maverick: Your seven minutes are up, Kitten. Are you ready to play?

The moment she had been waiting for with equal doses of excitement and fear was upon her. Glancing up at the webcam aimed down at her like a disapproving parent, Catarena took her fingers off the keyboard and tapped them nervously on her desk. She knew Maverick wanted to be in control, but what would he do if she countered his command.

There's only one way to find out, she thought, and placed her hands back on the keyboard.

BlackCat: As ready as I'll ever be.

Maverick: I want you to get up from the desk and bring the toys over to the computer, if you haven't already done so.

BlackCat: You didn't instruct me to.

She answered cockily, weighing the silver choker hugging her neck with the tip of a finger. If he wanted to try this power-play stuff, then she was willing to play along.

Maverick: So true, but for some reason I don't think you're saying that as meekly as you'd like me to think you were.

Catarena's eyes widened in surprise and she let out a little chuckle. He definitely had her figured out.

BlackCat: It's the truth. You didn't.

Maverick: Well, I'm telling you to do it now.

Getting up, Catarena went into her closet and pulled down the shoebox she had stashed in the back and took the lid off. She eyed the toys warily, blushing as her eyes slid across her buddy from the other night—if that night was any reference, she was sure she'd be blushing again.

BlackCat: I'm back.

Maverick: Good, Kitten. I take it you received your camera.

BlackCat: Yes, but you took an awful big risk. There wasn't any guarantee it would work with my computer.

Maverick: It's top of the line, it works for almost all computers. It was a calculated risk, but one I'm sure will pay off.

BlackCat: We'll see.

Maverick: Did you run the program and get it installed correctly.

Catarena took a deep breath and popped her knuckles, trying to relieve all the added built-up pressure. It was time.

BlackCat: Yes.

Maverick: Time to come out of the dark, Kitten. Turn it on.

Glancing back up at the camera, Catarena bit her bottom lip apprehensively and thought to herself, *here goes nothing*.

BlackCat: No. You first.

The woman could test the patience of Job himself. Mason rubbed the back of his neck. She was a challenge, but one he was ready and willing to meet head-on.

Maverick: Kitten, you aren't listening again. How I wish you were here so I could put you over my knee and teach you a lesson in listening and following directions.

BlackCat: For some reason, I don't think you're joking.

Maybe she was finally starting to get it. Mason wanted her to understand him. He needed for her to want to please him just as much as he wanted to please her. To give herself freely. To please not only him but herself.

Maverick: You're researching BDSM and control is a big part of it. If you aren't willing to give it over, this will never work and we could very well be wasting both of our times.

Mason let his words sink in for a moment before he added more.

Maverick: I may not own a vast assortment of floggers and the like—I prefer the flat of my hand to anything else—but I can help you understand firsthand how dominant, everyday men handle control issues. Make up your mind—the decision is yours.

Mason waited for a sign. Anything that would tell him what she was thinking, a question, anything. But nothing came. His cursor blinked tauntingly but no words appeared.

With his eyes closed, Mason tipped his head back against the chair. He exhaled the breath he'd been holding and prayed he'd be able to let her go if she decided not to respond.

A sound came from his computer speaker causing his heart rate to speed up to double-time. A small box asking him to view the webcam of BlackCat appeared. This is it, Mason thought to himself.

He wanted to see her, to know she was following his instructions. But a small part of him had warned against getting too close. A whisper of a thought cautioned Mason that to do so could be dangerous to his life as he knew it. So he'd instructed his Kitten to turn the lights out, opting for lit candles instead. He'd done the same.

After clicking the proper button to view BlackCat's webcam, Mason watched and waited for what was to happen next. It didn't take long before another box appeared on his computer screen and in it was a room backlit with what appeared to be dozens of candles.

The camera appeared to move and instead of seeing the room he'd briefly glimpsed, he now had the magnificent view of a beautifully nude woman who was cast in shadow from the shoulders up.

Her dark hair billowed around her like a gathering storm. He could just see the peaks of her nipples through the long, curly strands. Her hair looked alive as it flowed over her shoulders and past the view of the camera. Mason could picture it pooled in her lap. He couldn't help but comment.

Maverick: With hair as beautiful as yours, I bet I'd recognize you anywhere.

BlackCat: I've always loved it too, but sometimes it's such a hassle that I think about cutting it.

The thought of her beautiful hair being chopped off made Mason see red.

Maverick: Cut your hair and you'll have me to deal with.

BlackCat: What is that supposed to mean?

Maverick: It means you'll finally get firsthand experience on spankings and learn there is a big difference between those meant for erotic pleasure and those meant for punishment.

BlackCat: Is that a threat?

Maverick: No, Kitten, it's a promise and you're running out of time.

Mason expected some type of question as an opening but, once again, she managed to surprise him.

BlackCat: I wanted you to see how well I can follow directions. I'm sorry if I made it so you don't want to help me anymore, but this is new and I'm extremely uncomfortable.

Mason wanted to gather her in his arms and hold her nude body, stroking every delectable inch of her flesh until she was calm and comfortable with his gaze.

Maverick: You have nothing to apologize for, Kitten, and although I'll push, I'll never make you feel anything less than the beautiful woman you are.

And beautiful she was. He might not be able to clearly see her features due to the low angle of the camera, but her body was natural and beautiful. She tossed her hair back giving him a clear view of the shiny silver choker he'd sent along with the toys. Seeing his brand of ownership clasped so perfectly around her neck made all the blood in his body surge to his already erect cock.

Mason's eyes drifted lower, taking in her chest and below. Her breasts were full with dark, round tips puckered in anticipation. The dip of her waist flared to healthy hips Mason could imagine holding onto as he thrust into her body from behind.

The way she stayed stock-still proved the discomfort she'd just admitted to. All of a sudden, Mason wanted to do whatever was necessary to put her at ease.

Maverick: You are beautiful, Kitten.

Mason typed the simple compliment, wishing he could convey more.

BlackCat: Thank you.

Although she was still sitting in semidarkness, Mason saw her taut body visibly relax at his words. He made a promise to himself to praise her beauty at every chance he had. He never wanted his Kitten to doubt what he thought of her.

Maverick: Do you want me to turn on my webcam or are you more comfortable with me viewing you only?

Her return message came instantly.

BlackCat: Oh, no, you don't. I want to see you too!

Maverick: Your wish is my command, Kitten. At least this time, so here you go.

Mason typed the words as he sent an invitation to view his webcam over the Internet. It was a strange sensation knowing he was being watched.

BlackCat: I can hardly see you.

Mason figured it was for the best since he was extremely aroused and had no intention of covering up with more than the drawstring pajama bottoms he was wearing.

Maverick: That's the plan, for now at least.

BlackCat: Oh, okay.

The words flashed before him and for a moment, Mason was surprised a barrage of questions hadn't immediately followed.

Maverick: The candlelight may be casting shadows, Kitten, but I can clearly see your body. Your breasts are just as I'd imagined them.

Nothing followed but a pink-cheeked smiley icon. She was embarrassed by his praise, it seemed. Mason decided it was time to push a bit more.

Maverick: Caress them for me, baby. Pretend it's my hands on you.

Mason waited with bated breath to see if she would do it. When she did, his cock throbbed in protest. He palmed its cloth-covered length and prayed for strength to hold out.

The sight of her hands softly fondling her breasts was so erotic Mason couldn't believe he hadn't thought to get them webcams earlier.

Maverick: Beautiful, absolutely beautiful. Arouse yourself, Kitten. Pinch your nipples. Roll them between your fingers. Show me what you like.

Not being able to see her face was torture. Did she have her eyes open? Every once in a while she'd dip down just enough so he could clearly see her mouth. The way she kept her lower lip clamped tightly between her white teeth made him long to do a bit of nibbling himself. Just thinking it made him want to give up the whole idea of remaining anonymous.

Maverick: If you've got a desk light, I want you to turn it on and angle it down. Then sit back and open your legs for me, Kitten. Let me see how pretty you are.

Mason thought he'd swallow his tongue when she did as he asked. Without so much as a typed message in protest, she flicked a small lamp on. She then leaned back in her chair adjusting her hips forward so he had a wonderful shot of her.

The way she was rolling her nipples between her fingers made him wonder if she perhaps enjoyed a bit of pain with her pleasure. Would she enjoy it if he were right there scraping his teeth over the sensitive nubs, tugging and pulling as he sucked them relentlessly into his mouth?

Moisture glistened across her pubic mound. Her trimmed hair left just enough to the imagination to have him on the edge of his seat. The way the dark thatch of hair contrasted against the creamy, pale flesh of her thighs had him reaching for the drawstring of the pajama bottoms he was wearing.

The pink lips of her pussy were glistening with her essence. Mason longed to lap at her entrance, to taste the thick cream of her arousal. Would her breathy moans be as arousing as those in his dreams?

Mason watched as she shifted. For a brief, panicked moment, he thought she was going to shut down the connection. Instead, she sent him a message.

BlackCat: I need 2 cum.

Maverick: Not yet, Kitten. Did you follow my earlier instructions? All of them?

BlackCat: Y

Mason smiled at her answer. She was typing as little as possible, which meant she was very close.

Maverick: Good girl. Then just sit back and follow instructions. Do you understand?

BlackCat: Y

Maverick: The first thing I want you to do before I let you come is remove the pleasure balls you've been holding inside of you.

Mason palmed the length of his now free, erect shaft. There was no way in hell he could watch his Kitten get off, her body glistening, without helping himself along. He followed with his eyes as one of her hands left her breast and made the journey south.

Inhibitions forgotten, she ran a single finger up her slit. He watched in erotic fascination as she removed first one of the pink orbs and then the other. The way her body flowered open, her cream covering the balls made his mouth water. How he wished he could taste her, smell the musk of her essence as she brought herself to the pinnacle then shattered in sweet abandon.

BlackCat: Now?

Maverick: I'll tell you when, Kitten. Grab the vibrator now. Run it over your nipples first and then down to your pretty little pussy.

She let the pleasure balls slide from her fingers to the floor. She appeared to be breathing heavily but made no move to do as he asked. Her body looked to be covered in a thin sheen of perspiration. Mason was dying to taste her, would do anything to be able to run his tongue along her flesh, licking and teasing until she was begging for relief. When she just sat there, doing nothing, Mason prompted her to continue.

Maverick: The vibrator. Right now, baby.

Her hands reached up to gather her hair. Her movements brought her into the light a bit better, although not well enough to see her clearly. When she had her hair wound on the top of her head, she grabbed a pencil off the desk and stuck it through her hair to hold it into place.

Mason thought to scold her for her actions because he loved watching her long hair as is caressed her body with every movement she made, but he had second thoughts when he saw the outline of her neck circled in silver.

It looked delicate and sexy, like a place he could rasp his afternoon stubble across, making her wet and ready in the process. Mason could imagine the feel of her warm, giving flesh against his lips as he suckled her, leaving his mark.

He could see her lips move as she ran the tip of the blue vibrating toy across her nipples. Would it be breathy moans or explicit cries slipping from her mouth? Mason decided it was time to point out exactly how arousing the sight of her pleasuring herself was. To do so, he stood and dropped his pants, completely freeing his cock. He sat back at his computer then sent her another message.

Maverick: I want you to move the vibe lower now, Kitten, and watch me on your screen. I don't think you understand quite how much you turn me on.

She slowly, teasingly ran the toy down her abdomen, her hand stilling briefly when she looked up, more than likely expecting more erotic directions from him. What he wouldn't give to be able to look straight into her lust-induced eyes. Would her lids be heavy or would she have her eyes closed? The thick fringe of her lashes protecting her from the outside world as her mind and body spun out of control?

Maverick: Yes, baby, look what you do to me. Watch me while I watch you, knowing it's all for you. It's as if your soft hand is stroking me instead of my own. I'll be thinking how it would be to have you on your knees in front me with your lips and tongue pleasuring my cock.

His own words in combination with his body movement had him on the edge in no time. Watching her move the vibrator over her body pushed him even further and for a moment, Mason wasn't sure he'd be able to hold on. It was time.

She leaned down for better access, the vibrator disappearing between her folds, and for a second Mason thought she looked familiar. There was something about the way she held her head, the angle of her neck that made him pause but it was quickly forgotten when he felt as if he would explode any minute.

Maverick: Now, Kitten. Come for me now.

Chapter Six

 howcontent

This had to be the single most arousing thing she had ever done in her entire life. Knowing Maverick was watching her was so intense Catarena didn't know how much longer she would be able to last. The toys, the camera, the whole damn thing was bringing her closer and closer to the most intense orgasm she'd ever felt in her entire life.

When his words flashed on the screen giving her permission to come, her body responded to his command, causing her to arch up onto the vibrator. Pushing it as deep inside her trembling body as possible, she came violently for him to see. Catarena's body shook and her nipples grew more taut than they had ever been before, as her body rocked against the wave sweeping her under.

Shaking and trembling, Catarena moved the still pulsing vibrator from between her legs and reached for the keyboard. There were so many different things she wanted to say, so many different things she wanted to do, but she could only peck out two little words.

BlackCat: Thank You.

Maverick: I want you to watch me, Kitten. Watch me as I come for you now. It's all for you.

The camera view began to change, quickly moving up the muscular chest to a strong jawline all the way up until Maverick's face was finally on the screen.

"Oh, my God," she screamed, as the face of her boss came into view. Catarena reached up and yanked the wire from the camera, immediately disconnecting his web view when she realized she'd been sitting up in full view of the camera.

Sitting back down, she stared at the screen in complete shock. What was she going to do? The person responsible for the most intense orgasms she'd ever had, the one who had begun to awaken her from her sexual slumber, was the same man who signed her paychecks.

Maverick: What happened?

Catarena placed her fingers on the keyboard but quickly removed them. She didn't know what to say. *Sorry, sir, I can't play anymore, I have to get up early in the morning to deliver your mail,* didn't seem appropriate.

Maverick: Kitten, are you there?

Maverick's face stared at her from the screen, frowning and confused. Catarena could see him looking toward the camera giving her an eagle-eye view of the man whose mail she delivered on a daily basis. It was almost comical, the way he was looking into the computer, as if he were trying to see inside, to her.

Hands trembling, Catarena pulled them away from the keyboard. She knew she had to say something. She was just having a hard time coming up with anything. Quickly grabbing her robe from off the floor, Catarena covered her body. She was embarrassed, she was ashamed, she was so freaking fired.

"Oh, my God. Oh, my God. Oh, my God," she repeated over and over again as she quickly tied the sash around her shivering body. Nervously, Catarena bit down on her thumbnail and watched the screen, as if afraid Maverick...no not Maverick—Mason Broderick—was going to jump through the screen.

There was a buzz from her Instant Message box startling her. It was quickly followed by a sentence typed in bold shaded letters.

Maverick: **Damn it, BlackCat, answer me!**

The pounding of her heart was almost as loud as the buzz from her Instant Message box. Everything was going to be okay, she promised herself as she placed her hands to the keyboard and nervously responded.

BlackCat: I'm here.

Maverick: What happened? Are you okay?

Hell, no, I'm not okay, she said to herself, almost laughing at his words. She was about to have a nervous breakdown and he wanted to know if everything was okay.

"Hey, honey, I'm home," Bailey called from outside of her bedroom door, jarring Catarena into action.

BlackCat: I have to go, my roommate just came home.

Maverick: You have a roommate?

BlackCat: Yes.

Maverick: Male or female?

There's no time for this, she thought, frantically trying to quickly bring the session to a close.

BlackCat: Female.

Maverick: Well, she has lousy timing. I think I'm going to hurt for hours.

BlackCat: I'm sorry. I really have to go.

Maverick: *sigh* It's okay, Kitten. Let's meet tomorrow.

BlackCat: I can't.

Maverick: Why?

Panicked, Catarena scrambled for an answer. She was never good at lying, never had been — not even as a kid — and now, when she really needed a reason, nothing came to mind.

BlackCat: I have prior plans.

Maverick: Well, what about Friday then?

BlackCat: I can't.

Maverick: What's going on here?

BlackCat: Nothing. I have to go.

That was just going to have to do. Moving the mouse, Catarena clicked on the X button in the box ending their conversation. She then moved it quickly to the bar, disconnecting her Instant Message and threw the cordless mouse across the room, chipping her lilac paint in the process.

"Fuck!" Catarena bellowed at the top of her lungs. Jumping up she unlocked her door and yanked it open, dashing out of her room. She ran down the hallway, skidding to a stop in front of a dazed Bailey who was pouring a glass of orange juice. "Oh, my God. Oh, my God. Oh, my God."

"'Hello' will suffice," Bailey said amused, setting the container on the counter. "What's your problem? Did his wife come home in the middle of your little rendezvous?"

Gulping, Catarena took a deep breath and replied shakily, "He's not married."

"So he says?" Bailey countered disbelieving. Turning around, she walked to the cabinet and grabbed another glass for Catarena.

"Oh, I know."

"How do you know?"

"Because he's our boss."

Bailey paused, putting the juice back on the counter in the middle of pouring. An amused look crossed her face as she said, "You mean Satan."

"No," Catarena said, shaking her head slowly. She was still having a problem coming to grips with what had just happened. "I mean our boss boss."

The last look of humor fell slowly from Bailey's face. "You mean..."

"Yes. I mean Mason Broderick of Broderick, Inc."

"Shut. Up."

"I'm not lying." The last bit of steam she had left slipped out of her as she dropped onto the barstool, trying to catch her breath. It was as if everything were happening in slow motion. This couldn't be happening. There was no way her Maverick was the same Maverick Wall Street bragged on. The same man who controlled a billion-dollar industry was the same man who had been controlling her orgasms. It just didn't add up.

"Maybe you were mistaken." Bailey tried hopefully, with a sick look on her face.

"I'm in his office all the time, Bay."

"But webcams are fuzzy. It could be anyone."

"It's him, Bailey. Trust me. It's him."

Bailey shook her head and turned and walked out of the room. "Where are you going?" Catarena called after her. There was no way she could face this alone.

Bailey returned a few seconds later with a bottle of tequila they kept in a cheap-looking bar globe in the living room. Pouring the liquor into the remaining room of Catarena's glass, Bailey handed the drink to Catarena then filled her own. Pulling another stool around the counter, Bailey sat down and lifted the glass for a toast. "We are so fucking fired."

"We? Since when did you get fired too?"

Taking a long drink from her glass, Bailey looked over at Catarena and replied. "You know they always blame the black girl and, come on, as if I'm going to work for Satan by myself. I don't think so."

"What am I going to do?"

"Did you have your camera on?"

"Yes."

"Was it pointed at your face?"

Catarena could feel herself beginning to blush. "Some of the time."

"Do you think he recognized you?"

"I don't know." Catarena moaned, dropping her hands into her lap. "Maybe, he didn't say anything, but he could have."

"He employs thousands of people."

"True, but I'm the one who gets stuck bringing him his mail."

"But normally you deal with The Dragon Lady."

"But what if—"

"No 'buts'," Bailey said firmly. "If he recognized you, he would have said so. You're worrying for nothing. Just wear your hair different when you go up there and sunglasses or something, and he won't know it's you."

My hair, Catarena thought, bringing her hand up to her dark tresses. He loved her hair, in fact, had even told her this night he would recognize it anywhere. "I have to cut it."

"Have you lost your mind?" Bailey bellowed, shocked. Catarena hadn't cut her hair in the last ten years, only trimming it on rare occasions. "No, you won't."

"Yes, I have to, Bay. He'll notice it." Getting up from her stool, she moved around the counter and pulled open the mess drawer, extracting the scissors from within. Catarena walked out of the kitchen, straight into the bathroom and stared at her shockingly white face in the mirror. What had she done? Her damn curiosity had really gotten her into it this time.

Taking a deep breath, Catarena pulled out the pencil, allowing her dark hair to spill around her like a stormy cloud. With tears pooling in her eyes, she grasped the end of her hair and brought the scissors up to it when Bailey's hand gripped hers.

"Why are you doing this?" Bailey asked, tightening her hold on Catarena's hand.

"Because he'll notice."

"Why will he notice your hair?"

"Because he likes long hair. Come on, how many women do you know who have hair down to their rear?"

"None, if you cut yours."

"Bailey, this isn't up for discussion. If he finds out that it's me, I'll die of embarrassment. Money Mason and the mailroom girl. Could it be any more sitcom than that?"

Bailey took the scissors out of Catarena's hand and finished the last of her drink. Setting the empty glass down on the counter, she pushed Catarena down onto the vanity stool and turned her away from the mirror.

"This is crazy, but I'm going to help simply for the 'told you so' factor that's bound to come from it. And besides you can't even cut a straight line. I'm not going to let you mess up your hair."

"Thank you," Catarena murmured, looking straight ahead. Just because she knew it had to be done, didn't mean she wanted to watch it happen.

"So are we talking about butch Demi Moore *Ghost* haircut, or *Zorro* Catherine Zeta-Jones haircut?"

"Catherine."

"Wise choice," Bailey said, as she stepped behind Catarena. "The first cut's always the worst."

"That's what they all say."

* * * * *

Close to a week had passed by without so much as a single email from BlackCat and it was driving Mason crazy. God knows he was angry enough to throttle her with his bare hands when he finally found her. And he would find her. It was just a matter of time.

With a dark scowl furrowing his brows, Mason sent another email to his mystery woman. He'd lost count of how many messages he'd sent the past week. He'd even written letters and mailed them to her. At first, he'd tried to be comforting, wanting her to know he was worried, but as the days trickled by at a snail's pace, he'd become angry and his anger only seemed to grow.

His last letter was one of sheer dominance. He was ordering her to get in touch with him. It was probably the most stupid thing he'd done, but he couldn't seem to help himself. The only other thing he could think of was to hire a private investigator. At this point, he wasn't beyond using every available means of tracking his Kitten down. And when he finally found her, they were going to have it out once and for all. It bothered Mason that he knew no more about BlackCat than the city where she lived. At least her post office box information would give the private investigator a place to start.

Mason glanced at his desk. The list he'd been working on didn't seem nearly as long as it should. He'd taken to making a list of everything he knew about her, which didn't amount to much, but it was a start.

"Better than nothing," he mumbled to himself as he lifted the phone from the base on his desk.

It was almost time for him to go home, but just as it had been before he'd met her in the chat room, Mason was working late. He had no real reason to rush back to his place as he'd done every night for the past week in hopes she would contact him.

Mason grasped the cordless phone in his hand so tight his knuckles turned white. Too anxious to stay seated, he quickly rose from his chair to pace the length of his office while he dialed Sebastian's number into the handset.

"Yeah?" a drowsy voice grumbled.

"Did you find anything?" Mason asked without apology, even though he was calling late.

An exasperated sigh came through the phone line. "Not everyone works all hours of the night. You've been running me ragged, I need sleep, Mason."

"And I need to find her, dammit!" Mason exploded.

"I'm a lawyer, Mason. I may tinker with computers but I am by no means a hacker or anything remotely close. I opened an account and spent half the evening with some of the freakiest people imaginable on the website you gave me. Not once did she show up."

Mason wanted to punch something. He wasn't normally a violent man, but right now he was feeling more like a possessive animal than a human. "It's good for her that she wasn't there," he growled.

"Good God, man! Listen to yourself. She wasn't there. I sent a message to the email address you gave me and even tried to get on her Instant Messenger list with no luck. Sorry, man, but I couldn't find her."

"I'll find her." The words sounded ominous even to his own ears.

"Mason—" Sebastian started, but Mason quickly cut him off.

"Thanks, Sebastian. I'm sorry I woke you." He hung the phone up with the flick of a finger then proceeded to heave it across the room where it landed against the wall with a dull thud. He then grimaced at his childish behavior.

It was after midnight when Mason finally left the office making his way home. It didn't matter how much he thought it over, he still couldn't come up with a reason she would call the whole thing off.

Over and over, night after night, he thought about their last meeting. Things had seemed to be going so well and even though he hadn't really considered doing it previously, Mason had all but made up his mind the two of them would have to meet in person and soon.

The feelings to wash over him after glimpsing her features, after seeing the glow of her skin backlit by a roomful of burning candles, had been too much. Never in his life had he felt such a strong pull toward a woman.

Never in a million years would he be able to get the vision of her long hair hanging freely over her nude chest. The way she'd nibbled her bottom lip, drawing it tautly between her teeth would forever remain imprinted in his mind.

There was something about the way she moved. Something about the swanlike arch of her neck after she'd twisted her hair up in a bun, securing it to her head with a pencil as if it were second nature.

The way she moved seemed familiar. His inability to place her was driving Mason crazy. He needed to figure out what it was about her that made her seem so familiar.

The slight niggling sensation in the back of his mind was part of the reason his nights were sleepless and his days were filled with remembering the tiniest of details about her. Things she might have said, clues as to who she was.

She even haunted his dreams. There was nothing more frustrating than finally drifting off to sleep only to wake up right on the edge of discovering who she was. It was as if his subconscious mind were demanding he recognize her but his conscious mind wasn't cooperating.

It was frustrating as hell! And it seemed everyone around him from the top executives of Broderick, Inc. down to the doorman were all aware of his fierce mood. They'd all been evading him as much as possible. So, not only was the cyber witch messing with his personal life but she was messing with his business.

Once home, Mason showered and changed. He knew it was no use but couldn't help himself. Warily, he booted up his computer and checked his email. His heart almost lodged in his throat when he realized he had a new message from BlackCat.

"This had better be good, Kitten," he said with deadly calm as he clicked to open the short but to-the-point missive.

Maverick,

I'm sorry if I've worried you. It wasn't fair of me to do so after all of your help so I've decided to contact you one last time to let you know I am fine. Please don't try to contact me anymore. Something has come up and whatever this was between the two of us just isn't possible any longer.

I'm truly sorry,

BlackCat

"Son of a bitch," he cursed into the silent room. Rereading the email, Mason searched for a hidden message, anything to give him a clue as to who she was and why she'd cut out on him.

"We'll see, Kitten, We'll see," Mason said the words in the stillness of the room, but made no effort to answer her message.

There had to be a reason why she'd pulled the plug on their relationship and he was going to find out what it was if it was the last thing he did. Mason strode straight to his room.

The night was long and restless with thoughts of a dark-haired vixen spinning in and out of his dreams. At one point, Mason woke up with his cock so hard he thought he'd explode. Visions of his Kitten hovering over him in bed taunted him mercilessly. The vivid dreams of her mouth on his rigid shaft, her hair swirling around him, pooling in his lap while he burrowed his hands deeply in the silky strands, only made matters worse. And if that wasn't bad enough, he couldn't seem to bring himself out of it. When his dream became even clearer, her climbing atop him, straddling his thighs as his throbbing shaft rubbed at her wet slit, Mason wished himself awake, but the Dream Master was being a ruthless bastard this night.

And then he caught a glimpse of shiny white teeth biting into a full lower lip and couldn't help but hold his breath in anticipation. Maybe she would finally show herself. It was as if he were watching a movie behind the closed lids of his eyes, only every one of his senses was on alert and he could feel as well as see all that was happening.

When she lifted her hips, taking just the head of his cock into the entrance of her fist-tight pussy, he thought he would swallow his tongue. The way she lowered herself slowly, taking him in inch by inch was enough to steal all his control, Mason groaned even in his sleep.

She was so tight and so wet and all for him. Mason wanted to grab her hips and drive up into her, sheathing his entire length in one single lunge but he couldn't do it. He wouldn't move a muscle for fear the woman of his dreams might stop and he couldn't have that, she was too close to showing herself and Mason had to know who she was or risk insanity.

In the blink of an eye, she dropped down onto him, completely engulfing his length in her waiting body. Her action sent him spiraling over without warning, breaking the spell in the process.

Mason sat bolt upright in bed breathing heavily. A string of curses left his mouth at the lost vision only to be closely followed by even worse when he realized he'd had the granddaddy of wet dreams, fucking up his bed and his clothes in the process.

That was all it took for him to make the decision. Tomorrow, if need be, he would hire someone to find her, even if for no other reason than to spank her ass for worrying him all week.

Chapter Seven

ॐ

So far so good. Catarena let out another sigh of relief as her day came closer to the end. It had been a week since she'd last spoken to Mav…Mason, and it had been the longest most nerve-racking week of her life. Because everything was making her jumpy. She was constantly looking over her shoulder and dodging anyone and everyone who remotely resembled Mason. It was actually rather surprising how many dark-haired men over six-feet tall worked in her company. It would probably be pretty funny if it wasn't slowly driving her insane.

Rolling her metal cart to the back of the supply room, Catarena closed her eyes briefly saying a silent pray to St. Jude, the patron of loss causes, to help her out just a bit longer. After a week of nightly bombardments of emails, IMs and letters, Mason had finally stopped. Catarena didn't know if it was because he was upset or if he had just given up on her, either way, the longer she hid out, the more likely it would be for him to forget her. It wasn't what she really wanted, it was just what was best for everyone all the way around.

There was no way in the world Catarena would fit into his world, no more so than he would be able to fit into hers. Hell, she barely fitted into his cyber world. Girls like her never ended up with men like him. It just didn't happen in real life. Catarena didn't want to chance the fact Mason wouldn't want her once he knew who she really was. Online, she could have been anyone she wanted, but this was the real world. No booting up, no back key to erase the errors and no log-on names to hide behind.

Everything had worked out for the best, she kept trying to tell herself and she believed it…some of the time. Because when she wasn't busy dodging him, she was missing him. Which seemed strange in its own right, because she'd never really had him. Not the way he'd had her.

Catarena couldn't deny that Maverick had tapped into something inside her she'd never dreamed of. Something that had her craving his virtual touch as much as she craved his commands. Never before had she thought she would be open for that kind of control, the mind control that allowed him dominance over her body and soul.

And even after she ended all contact, she still kept the one physical contact of their time together that meant the most. She wore his collar with pride—even if no one else saw it—at night in her bedroom. She needed to keep it as a link to what they'd once had and what could never be.

"Putting up your cart already?" asked a weaselly voice from behind her. Catarena took a deep, calming breath before slowly turning around. The way her nerves were right then, one wrong word from Stan and she would blow her top.

"It's empty," she pointed out calmly.

Raising a condescending brow over an equally condescending stare, Stan moved into the middle of the doorway, blocking Catarena's exit. He was a small man—barely coming up to Catarena's shoulder—with a big ego, and like most tiny men, he had the biggest inferiority complex she had ever seen. Stan was a bully, more than likely had always been one since childhood. He was short, rude and entirely too evil to live.

"Not anymore." Smirking, he dangled a package in his stubby hand.

The urge to roll her eyes was hard to resist, but Catarena somehow managed, as she held out her hand for the package. Stan refused to come closer, extending his hand out to her, waiting for her to come to him. It was a power game and she was in no mood to play.

"Where does it go?" Catarena asked, as she moved closer to him.

"To the top."

Freezing, Catarena dropped her hand unable to believe her dramatic turn for the worse. "Mason's office?" she questioned, hoping she had misunderstood him.

Stan's eyebrow rose mockingly as he shoved the package at her. "So it's 'Mason' now, is it? I didn't know you and Mr. Broderick were on such friendly terms."

"We're not." Cursing herself for her blunder, Catarena took the package in her cold hand. "It is his name, isn't it?"

"You tell me?" he taunted.

Catarena wanted nothing more than to bash the troll over the head with the box. "Look, can't someone else do it? I'm not feeling very well and I think I need to go lay down."

"No, missy, someone else can't do it. *We* all work around here, and if you still want to be able to say the same, I suggest you saunter your little butt up there and pronto."

"I—"

"And I mean you, not your little friend. Don't think I haven't noticed how you're pawning most of your work onto her this week. Not all of us are so lucky to have friends pull our weight."

For some reason, Catarena seriously doubted Stan had friends, and it wasn't all her work, just anything that had to go to Mason's office. "I really need to go lay down," she tried again.

"If you want to go I can't stop you —" Catarena almost smiled in relief " — but if you go home, don't plan on coming back tomorrow."

Why the evil little stump, he'd probably been waiting all day with the package, just one more hoop he wanted her to jump through. She was highly tempted to tell him where he could put the package, but until she published her books, she was going to need a steady income. The only comforting thought was people like him always got what they deserved. Always.

"Fine," she bit out, clenching her teeth as he smirked at her answer. Stepping back, Stan turned to the side and gestured with his extended hand for her to leave. Narrowing her eyes, she shoved past him, loathing touching him, but wanting more than anything to be out of his presence.

Catarena walked down the aisle, pausing in front of Bailey's station looking for her friend, but to her luck and the testament of the way her day was going, Bailey wasn't there. Looking around, she searched the office for Bailey, but only spotted Stan standing exactly where she'd left him, staring at her. Not knowing what else to do, Catarena grabbed a pen off Bailey's desk along with her friend's reading glasses, and headed for the elevator. Shoving the button in, she groaned when it automatically opened. Almost as if it had been waiting for her.

Catarena stepped into the empty elevator and turned around just in time to see Stan give her a little sarcastic wave. Unable to resist, she waved back, but with just her middle finger. His look of utter disbelief was worth the slight chance she had of being fired. Pushing the package between her legs, she turned and slid the glasses on her pert nose. It made a difference but not much, so she took her dark tresses into her hands and put them up with the pen she had taken from Bailey's cubicle.

Her hair actually looked great, seeing how she had gotten it cut at Bailey's Chop N' Shop bathroom hair salon. Catarena had forgotten how rewarding it was to have shorter hair. It was less of a hassle and much easier to deal with. She guessed she owed Mason a thank you for the unintentional prompt to cut her hair, and for giving her enough fantasies to write about for a lifetime.

Checking out her reflection in the mirror through the blurry glasses, Catarena nodded her head, liking what she saw. In a knee-length mauve skirt and white blouse, she resembled a schoolmarm, especially with the glasses and the pen in her hair. No way resembling the erotic persona of BlackCat Mason had seen. If she was lucky, The Dragon Lady would be at her guard post and Catarena could do a drive-by, moving in and out, all before the elevators doors closed.

But then again, a part of her wanted to see him, even if it was just a parting glance. To see if he was okay, to see if he was… Sighing, Catarena shook her head, trying to clear it of all foolish thoughts. It was stupid to wish for something that would never be, no matter how much she wanted it.

The elevator slowed to a stop and Catarena's heart picked up a salsa beat, drumming quickly in her chest. Nervously she peered through the opening doors, moving her head to the side trying to glance around the office. Stepping out of the elevator, she rushed into the empty room, saying a silent thank-you prayer and dropped the package on top of the orderly desk.

She whirled around as she heard the inner office door opening and a voice spilling out into the room.

"Would you wait one second?" commanded The Dragon Lady. Catarena froze in her step, knowing she couldn't just dash into the elevator without arousing suspicion and ire. "We're finishing up a letter and you can take it down with you."

Fuck, she muttered to herself. It was definitely time to get a new saint. "I'm kinda in a hurry. This was my last delivery for the day." Turning around she faced Mrs. Garner with an apologetic look. "I'm officially off."

"Did you clock out yet?" she asked, crossing her arms across her chest.

"No."

"Then you're still on the clock. Don't worry, I'm sure Mr. Broderick won't mind the five minutes of overtime you'll be collecting."

Glancing nervously at the slightly parted door, Catarena knew she wasn't going to be able to slink out as she had hoped. "Just sit over there, and I'll get it to you in a few minutes."

"Yes, ma'am."

Mrs. Garner gave Catarena a firm nod before heading back into Mason's office. Sighing in despair, Catarena moved to the plush couch, which was pushed against the same wall the door was on, and sat down. It was the best choice, because if she sat there, Mason wouldn't be able to see her unless he came out of the office.

Nervously she tapped her foot on the thick carpet as she bided her time. It would be all right, she promised herself over and over again. Just a few more minutes and she'd be out of there, and Mason would be none the wiser. She could faintly hear the muted tones through the closed door, their voices mostly drowned out by the thick walls.

Catarena placed her hand against her rumbling stomach and tried to calm the butterflies flickering inside. The situation was literally making her feel sick. It was almost as if she were back in grade school, sitting outside of the principal's office waiting for her parents to come out.

The door pushed outward and Catarena instantly froze. Barely breathing, she held as still as possible as Mrs. Garner walked out of the office. Breathing a sigh of relief when she closed the door, Catarena jumped to her feet, startling the older lady.

"I guess you are in a rush," she commented with a frown as she made her way over to her desk. "Let me address this and you can be off."

Following her over to the desk, Catarena stood nervously as Mrs. Garner filled out the envelope. The door again opened just as she was passing the envelope to Catarena, and Catarena instantly turned her back to the door, accidentally shaking the pen out of her hair.

Her dark hair cascaded down upon her shoulders, blocking her face from Mason's view as he walked over to the desk.

"Don't forget to add this," Mason said, his deep voice rolling over her body, similar to the way his posts had. His voice sent shivers down her spine, caressing her in places his hands had never been. Catarena didn't want to move. It was as if being within arm's reach of heaven but not able to enter, almost to paradise but not quite.

Mason accidentally kicked the pen that had tumbled from her hair as he came to a stop at the desk and he automatically bent down to pick it up. Catarena sidestepped him to get out of his way, hoping he'd stay turned away from her. She could just make out his features through the curtain of her hair, and he looked almost as delicious as the last time she'd seem him, the time before winning out because he had been nude.

"I think you dropped this." he replied, standing back up with the pen extending it toward her.

"Thank you," she muttered softly, reaching out for the pen, but her hand came in contact with dead air. Looking up through the wave of her hair, her eyes widen when she saw the look on his face. Surprise and suspicion clouded his eyes, as he reached out and moved her hair from in front of her face. His hand lightly brushed her cheek as he tucked the strands behind her ear.

Biting her bottom lip anxiously, Catarena prayed he wouldn't recognize her but it was too late. The suspicion in his eyes quickly turned to anger as the clarity of who she was filled his face. Taking a step back, Catarena was about to bolt when Mason grabbed hold of her arm.

Pulling her back, he looked down into her upturned face and ran his eyes over her features, raking it all in. His eyes narrowed and his mouth tightened as he muttered angrily, "It's you."

Mason couldn't believe his eyes. With her dark, flowing hair, wide eyes and sickly pale face, his Kitten stood before him. The fact she looked so stricken was proof enough she knew who he was and probably had from the moment his webcam had landed on his face. The thought of her evading him, knowing full well who he was, made him irate.

Mason narrowed his gaze at his secretary. She stood stock-still as if she weren't sure what to do. "You're done for the day, Mrs. Garner. I'll take it from here."

"If you're sure, sir?" she answered with wide, watching eyes.

"I'm sure. I'll see you tomorrow."

Mason said the last as he tugged his Kitten through the door behind him. Once across the threshold, he nudged her farther into the room, taking advantage of her shocked demeanor. He was absolutely sure she wouldn't be as quiet or as malleable once she gathered herself back together.

After locking the door, Mason kept his back to her and took several deep breaths to try and settle his anger as well as the instant, overwhelming arousal to overtake him upon recognizing her. It only took a second to realize no amount of deep breathing was going to help.

"What's your name?"

His question must have caught her off guard. "W-what?" she stuttered.

"Your name," he growled. "Tell me your name. Now, Kitten."

Mason watched as she nervously licked her lips. The gesture wasn't meant to be erotic but it kicked his already pulsing libido into high gear.

"I...um...my name's Catarena. Catarena Vaughn."

Her hesitant answer made him want to roar in anger. Instead, he laughed. The mirthless sound wasn't meant to elicit a smile. It was mocking, biting, just the way he'd meant it. The way her chin came up a notch warned she could give as good as she got, which was fine with Mason. After all, he'd been spoiling for a fight all week.

"Cat." He let the single word roll across his tongue, testing the feel of it as it slipped from his lips. Shaking his head, he said, "I like 'Kitten' better so that's what I'll call you."

Her eyes narrowed to dangerous blue slits, her hands clenched into tight fists at her side. "You won't be calling me anything."

"You think so?" Mason taunted as he moved toward her. His slow, sure steps brought him easily to the center of the room where Catarena stood. Her eyes darted around the room as if she were looking for a way of escape but she didn't move an inch. Not so much as a flinch as he stopped mere inches from her. A new wave of respect bloomed in his chest but he pushed it ruthlessly away.

Mason closed the space between them, walking her backwards until she was up against his desk. Her eyes widened and she stepped to the side.

"I don't think so," he growled, leaning into her. When his lips were a breath away from hers, he said, his voice low, rough, "Do you know how long I've been wanting to do this, Kitten? How much time we could have had? Instead, I've been going insane wondering where you were, who you were with. It won't happen again, baby, that much I can promise."

Mason then proceeded to take her mouth in a hard, punishing kiss. He felt her body immediately stiffen against his, her hands pushed at his chest, but he wasn't going to relent.

"Open." The single-worded command was raw and lust-driven.

When she didn't do as he ordered, instead, trying to turn her head away from the kiss, Mason grasped her face in his hands. He nipped sharply at her lower lip. "Open."

When she did, he flicked his tongue past her lips, tasting the warm recess of her mouth as if he'd been starved for the contact. When her ineffectual struggles stopped and she melted into his chest, he slowed the kiss, gentled it, laving at her mouth, worshipping her lips.

Her submission did nothing to alleviate his anger and frustration. Breaking the kiss, Mason spun her around and moved her until she was lying facedown over his desk.

"Mason…"

"Ah, ah, ah, Kitten. You had your chance. We could have done this nice and sweet, but you went and hid, so it's my way," he growled, cutting her off as he lifted her skirt. With the flick of his wrist, Mason administered a stinging swat to her cotton-covered backside, startling a yelp out of her. "Don't ever hide from me again."

"Bastard," she hissed at him, but in the same breath, she placed her hands on his desk.

"Among other things," he said as he ripped her dainty, white lacy-style panties from her body. "It doesn't change the fact you'll be begging before I'm through, though."

Mason absorbed her startled gasp as if she'd just whispered sweet nothings in his ear as he unfastened his pants. With his cock throbbing, standing at attention, Mason was on her. His sank the full-length of his erection into her slowly, inch by inch, loving the noises she made.

The way her inner muscles quivered around him, trying in vain to accommodate his size. She was small and so hot he thought she would send them both up in flames. The feel of her tight sheath wrapped around his turgid length was even better than he'd imagined, better than his wildest, kinkiest dreams.

When he was buried to the hilt, the generous swell of her ass pressed tightly to his groin, Mason leaned over her back. Grasping her shortened length of hair in his hand, he moved it to the side then nipped the curve of her neck.

"I'll take the fact you cut your hair out of your delectable ass later. Right now though, I'm going to fuck you, Kitten, hard and fast until you scream my name. My name, do you hear me? Not some goddamned alias."

He pulled slowly from her tight sheath, her answering whimper music to his ears. While part of her may have submitted, she was still far from being docile.

"In your dreams, *Maverick*," she threw at him, taunting him with the use of his screen name. Her words ended on a whoosh of air as he plowed deeply into her, knocking the breath from her lungs.

"You'd probably run screaming if you knew what was in my dreams," he whispered the words in her ear, his voice menacing. "You've opened Pandora's box, baby."

Mason was done talking, done listening. Grasping her curvaceous hips, he started a slow, steady rhythm, taking her quickly to the top but never quite giving her enough to push her over.

Her breath was coming in sobbing gasps and Mason had to grit his teeth to hold back the powerful need to bring her off. He wanted nothing more than to feel the muscles to her cunt pulsate around his shaft but he wouldn't allow it just yet. First, she needed to understand who was in charge. Who would always be in charge.

With his jaw tight, holding back his own growing need for release, Mason quickened his pace, slamming his full-length home, deep and hard over and over again until she was chanting his name, grinding herself against the edge of his desk.

When Mason realized what she was doing, he pulled back, bringing her with him by the iron-tight hold he had on her hips.

"Dammit!" she cursed.

"I don't think so, baby. Not until you ask and I give permission."

"Fuck you!" Her voice was hoarse, breathless.

"You'd enjoy that, wouldn't you," he said, toying with her as he once again set a pace sure to keep her teetering on the edge.

It was only a matter of minutes before the words tumbled from her lips. "Oh, God. Please."

He was sure she was going to give kicking his ass a good try when he was done but, for now, he couldn't help the triumphant smile curving his mouth.

"Tell me," he growled the words, sinking deep into her inflamed body. Tiny spasms rocked her, grasping his cock in quick jerks. "Say it!"

"I need to come. Make me come, damn you!"

Mason thought it might be as close as he was going to get tonight. He powered into her while reaching around for the sensitive nub of her clit. It was all she needed to fly. Her body milked him as wave after wave flowed through her taut body. His name a scream on her lips as he followed.

Chapter Eight

&

Over the course of her lifetime, Catarena had been made love to, had engaged in sexual intercourse and had even been dry-humped in the back of a '74 Camero, but never in her life had she been so thoroughly fucked as she had been mere minutes ago. Maverick had truly lived up to his name and his boasts.

Still leaning forward, she tried to rise, but Mason remained bent over her. It wasn't the most ladylike position in the world but, then again, it wasn't very ladylike to let your wicked boss have his way with you over his desk. The cool feel of his zipper against her backside was a cold reminder of where they were and what they had just done. They had been in such a rush they hadn't even taken the time to undress. Catarena knew she should be ashamed, but she was too busy enjoying the effects of having his still firm cock in her body.

The mingled scent of their sex drifted between them, filling the room with their lustful aroma. Their combined essence was just as arousing as the feel of him still filling her. Catarena had only caught a passing glance at his penis on the cam, but from the way she felt stuffed full, she was willing to bet he was as big as his cyber namesake.

Involuntarily she clenched around him at the thought. Apparently, her body wasn't done with him quite yet. He was addicting, but not so addicting she could totally forget where they were. Giving a soft moan, she shifted, trying to silently signal him to move—she was too embarrassed to ask him.

Never in a million years would she have thought their meeting would end up like this. She had imagined sex, of course, but not mind-blowing, knee-numbing, having-to-sit-in-a-Jacuzzi-afterwards-to-soak-her-muscles sex. Closing her eyes, Catarena steadied her breathing, trying to take everything in. She wanted to remember every single detail, every single stroke, so she could use it in her novel. It may not be what she had planned, but Catarena wasn't going to waste the learning opportunity.

Mason eased up and slid his hand forward slowly, briefly gliding it along her clenched fist before slowly pulling out of her. Catarena flinched as he moved out of her sore body, but stayed where she was. She wanted to enjoy it to the last moment, because there was no way in hell it was going to happen again.

"We have some things to talk about," Mason said from behind her. Sighing Catarena eased up, not wanting to have this talk now.

"I can't think of anything we need to talk about," she remarked, sliding her skirt back in place.

"I can."

"Like—" Turning around, she faced Mason, and the cocky comment she was going to utter froze on her tongue as she felt the extra wetness between her legs that shouldn't have been there. "You didn't," she muttered horrified.

"Trust me, it wasn't planned," he replied dryly, handing her his handkerchief.

Of course, it wasn't planned. There was no way, Money Mason was going to intentionally have unprotected sex with a mailroom girl. Clenching his handkerchief in her hand, Catarena fought back tears, as she asked, "Where's your restroom?"

With hooded eyes, Mason watched her carefully as he pointed to a single door, almost hidden against the wall. As she pulled the door open, he replied calmly, "There isn't another way out of the bathroom, Kitten. I'll be waiting."

Catarena slammed the door childishly behind her and let out the suppressed scream she had wanted to let loose ever since she had first seen his face on her computer. It was easy to repair the damage they had done to her clothes and thighs, but trying to repair their messed-up relationship was something entirely different. Why couldn't he just be some freaking nerd who was barely legal, living in his grandma's basement? Oh, nooooo, when she fucked up, she really fucked up.

Looking in the mirror, she realized there was nothing she could do. She hadn't been sexually active in what felt like forever, hence the lack of hormonal control she had over her reproductive system. Quickly doing the math in her head, Catarena thought she might be safe, but wouldn't be willing to bet odds on it. She was Catholic. Two of her brothers had been conceived using the rhythm method.

A knock on the door drew her attention to problem number two. Unless she was willing to try to Spiderman her way up the building, she was going to have to face him. Shutting off the water, she took a deep breath and opened the door. Mason was leaning against his desk with his arms crossed, waiting for her.

Mason was once again his neat and orderly self, and if it hadn't been for the scent wafting in the air and the satisfied look glimmering in his eyes, anyone would have thought he was attending a meeting. Whereas Catarena looked as if she had been run over by a Mack truck. She was tired and sore and, Goddammit, she didn't have any underwear.

"I take it from the joyful face you made as you entered the bathroom that you're not on anything."

"I wasn't expecting to be attacked the moment I entered your office," Catarena said, jumping on the defensive.

His eyes narrowed as he pushed up from the desk. "You weren't attacked, but I'm willing to participate in any little fantasy you might want to act out."

"How about the 'I leave here and we forget this whole thing ever happened' fantasy."

"That's not a fantasy, Kitten, it's you dreaming." Mason walked toward her, slow and sleek, like a tiger stalking its prey. Catarena had to force herself not to retreat. She knew if he saw any signs of weakness, he would pounce. It was just in his nature. Stopping in front of her, Mason lifted his hand up to her hair and took a strand between his fingers. "I recall warning you not to cut your hair."

Okay, that sounded like a threat—a good threat—but a threat nevertheless. "I don't answer to you, Mason."

His jaw tightened as he released her hair. "That's where you're wrong. Last time I checked you are employed here, are you not?"

"As a mail clerk not as your personal whore," she spat. Catarena had to hold on to her anger. It was the only sane emotion she had left.

"Haven't you learned by now it's not wise to tempt me, Kitten? I'm liable to make you eat those words."

"I'd never be your whore."

"You make it seem so seedy," he remarked, sounding slightly amused.

"Fucking for money is."

"Fucking for pleasure isn't, though. I could make you crave me as much as you crave your next breath. To want to do things you never thought you would want to do. Experience things you didn't think were possible. You want to write a book. I can give you all the information you could ever need."

"I think I have enough research," she stated coolly, a hell of a lot cooler than she felt. Mason's words sent shivers down her body, making her worn-out libido perk up its tired head. Catarena had to get out of there before she did something she might regret—like stay. Turning, she went to leave when his words stopped her in her tracks.

"Why did you hide from me?"

"I think it's more than obvious, Mason. I didn't want you to know who I was."

"Why?"

"Because it's one thing to do those things with someone you'll never meet, but it's another thing to masturbate for the man who signs your paycheck. It was better when you were a stranger."

"I was never a stranger, Kitten. Not since the first night you let me in." Moving toward her again, Mason sidled up behind her and pulled her back against the length of his body. "And it's the way you like it. Admit it, Kitten. You liked me being in control, almost as much as I liked being in control."

Catarena would rather jump off a building than admit such a thing. "I think you're confusing interest with research."

Mason pulled her tighter into his body, nudging her hair out of his way and spoke softly into her ear. "I think you're the one confused, Kitten. You don't call the shots here. I do. Or did you forget?"

"Don't make me quit, Mason. I need this job."

"Then don't push me. You might have hidden from me for a little bit, but I promise you, Kitten, I would have found you." Taking her lobe between his teeth, Mason teased it gently with his tongue before biting down softly on it.

"Stop it." She all but meowed it. His rough, rumbled laughter in her ear let Catarena know she wasn't fooling him either. "I'll quit."

"And I'll give you the punishing spanking we were talking about," he warned, letting her go.

Catarena turned to him, refusing to be bullied. "This won't work, Mason, and when everything is said and done, I'll be the one holding the bag. I'll be just another woman who fucked her boss. My reputation might mean jack to you, but it's important to me." Not as much as it should have fifteen minutes ago when he was pounding in her from behind but it did matter. Catarena refused to be that girl.

"We're consenting adults, Kitten. Don't you think we're capable of having a personal relationship outside of work?"

Catarena gave a bitter chuckle. "Mason, we just had sex in your office, seconds after you asked me my name. Do you really think we can keep things businesslike at work?"

"It doesn't really matter whether we keep things businesslike or not. What matters is you coming to terms with the fact that you're mine."

She was going to try and leave both his office and him. Evidently she didn't understand just how determined he was. Not the type to back down, Mason was used to having his way. It wasn't a matter of moaning and groaning or pleading and begging to get what he wanted. That wasn't at all the way he worked.

He would take what he wanted by any means necessary with relentless resolve. The thought of her running, hiding from him, made red-hot anger bloom in his chest. He clenched his jaw against the need to drag her to his home and never let her leave.

Instead, he said, "If you try to hide again, Catarena, I'll come after you and it won't take me long to find you. Believe me, you won't like the consequences."

Mason hoped his use of her given name as well as the low, fierce tenor of his voice would make her think twice. When her eyes narrowed and her lips thinned in aggravation, he couldn't help but think how pretty she looked.

"Knock it off with the spanking crap, Mason, I'm not falling for it. I know you're a big, bad-assed businessman but I'm telling you, this won't work!"

She was perfect for him. Fierce and strong, and although Mason knew they would argue often, he also knew making up would be half the fun. His Kitten wasn't the type of woman to let a man run over the top of her, she'd keep him in line in a good way. Best of all, was the fact she wouldn't bore him to death like the giggling, clinging women his mother often tried to set him up with.

When she headed toward the door, Mason held himself stock-still so he wouldn't dive after her, but he couldn't allow her to leave without letting her know the score.

"You belong to me now, Kitten. Never forget it."

"I don't belong to you or anyone else, you arrogant ass." She didn't turn or look at him. The way she'd made the statement, with a cockiness proving how stubborn she was, rubbed him the wrong way. She was gloriously obstinate, something he'd never come across in a woman he was interested in. For the most part, women just fell at his feet. Mason didn't figure his Kitten would be doing the same anytime soon. That fact both irritated and intrigued the hell out of him.

Mason ignored her outburst. There would be time enough later to cure her of her naughty mouth. "I'll be by at eight in the morning to pick you up for work."

His words stopped her in her tracks. She whirled around, cheeks flushed, eyes flashing. Her mouth was no longer pinched tight in a straight line—it was gaping open.

"I won't go with you." Her words were calm but Mason detected just a slight quiver to her voice.

"Yes, you will."

He wanted to insist she belonged to him. He'd taken her over his desk like a madman and she hadn't complained — not really. Mason wanted her to know he would possess her every way possible there was for a man to possess a woman.

His cock ached at the thought of filling every orifice and making her beg for it, scream for it. Watching as Catarena headed for the door, Mason threw out one last reminder. "Eight o'clock, Kitten."

His words were answered with the banging crash of his office door slamming. Damn, she was beautiful when her feathers were ruffled. Mason chuckled then realized that for the first time in ages he felt alive, like a man who had more to look forward to than another sixteen-hour day at the office.

She'd be a hard one to crack but Mason was always up for a challenge. Getting to the prize was half the fun, and he had a feeling seducing Catarena Vaughan to his way of thinking was going to be a spectacular feat.

With deft fingers, Mason punched the needed numbers onto the keypad of his new phone. "West," a voice on the other end answered.

"Broderick here. I need the personnel file of a Catarena Vaughan sent to my office." Mason thanked Duncan West, one of his department supervisors, then hung up the phone.

Walking to the large picture window, he watched as the cars below raced up and down the street. The view of the skyline normally helped to soothe him, to put him at ease. Today, however, things were different. Today he was hot, and even though it hadn't even been an hour since he'd felt her pussy clasp his cock in its tight, pulsing heat, Mason was once again hard.

A curt knock announced the arrival of Catarena's file. Mason bid entrance to the man delivering it.

"Your file, sir," Duncan said, holding the file out with one hand.

"Thank you," Mason answered, taking the file. "Hold on just a minute and you can have it back."

He grabbed a pen and pad of paper off his desk then proceeded to take down the information he'd need to find Catarena Vaughan. After handing the file back, Mason left the office and headed for home, a determined smile curling his lips.

* * * * *

The next morning dawned bright and clear, Mason rubbed his hands together in anticipation. It was going to be an all-out war to get his Kitten in line to his way of thinking, but he wasn't worried in the least. Strategy was in his blood and he knew he could take anything the little hellion threw at him on the way to work.

He dressed as if on autopilot, just as he did every other morning, finishing with just enough time to make his way through traffic and to her apartment to pick her up. The only problem was, she wasn't home.

"What do you mean she's gone?" he growled at the attractive woman who answered the door. Catarena's roommate, he assumed.

"Just what I said... She's. Gone." The woman enunciated the words with slow lip motions as if he was dimwitted.

Mason wanted to rant and rave, but from the looks of the woman before him, he'd more than likely end up in jail if he did.

"And you are?" His patience was slipping, as was his voice. It had gone calm and low.

"Bailey," she said the word as if it was a given, offering no more.

Mason took a deep breath then released it. The woman — Bailey — looked familiar but he couldn't quite place her.

"Do you know where she went, Bailey?"

She nodded her head and then, just when he didn't think she was going to give him the much-wanted information, she said with a wicked twinkle in her dark brown eyes, "Said she had to go to work early, something about her asshole boss."

Bailey said the words, then with the snap of her wrist, the door closed in his face. Mason was speeding to the office, angry beyond belief when it clicked.

"The damned woman works for me," he grumbled the words then burst out laughing.

Seems Catarena and her friend had quite a lot in common. The one thing they won't have in common is going to be a sore ass, Mason thought brightly as he parked his car in the underground parking spot marked just for him.

Upon entering his office, Mason went directly for the intercom speaker next to his phone.

"Yes?" Mrs. Garner's voice came through the speaker.

"Connect me with the mailroom please."

"Right away, sir," she answered, and within minutes his desk phone was ringing.

Catarena might think she could evade him, but that wasn't going to happen, especially not on his time. She might even plan to hide before and after work as she had this morning, but Mason knew he wouldn't allow that either. "Nope, the sooner she comes to understand my terms, the easier it'll be for the both of us," he muttered the words to himself as he picked up the phone.

"Broderick."

"You called, sir?"

Mason knew damned well he was being an egotistical jerk but it made no difference. He meant to have his Kitten and he was willing to do anything to achieve his goal. "Has anything come in for me this morning?" he asked the question then smiled when he received an affirmative answer.

"Good. Very good. From now on, anything for me is to be delivered by Ms. Vaughan. Understood?"

There was complete silence on the other end of the line making Mason wonder what the problem was. He wasn't in the mood for any problems, he already had one live wire on his hands. He sure the hell didn't need any other employee problems on top of it.

Finally the man answered. "Uh, yes, sir, Mr. Broderick. Whatever you want."

"Good. Now tell me, did Ms. Vaughan come into work this morning?"

Once again silence.

"Yes, but she was several minutes late, which isn't entirely unusual for her." The voice held a cold edge as it spoke of Catarena.

"Send her here as soon as you've gathered my package."

"No problem, sir," was the answered reply as Mason hung up the phone.

Mason leaned back in his chair and waited, a triumphant smile on his lips. Catarena might think she could dodge him, but he had other plans. He'd become her shadow if need be. One way or another, he was going to become a huge part of her life, and she his. Getting there would be half the fun.

Mason heard voices outside his door and leaped from the chair. He cursed himself repeatedly for forgetting his watchdog of a secretary.

"Goddamn son of a bitch!" he berated himself, as he reached to open the door. A swirl of curly black hair was moving at a fast pace toward the elevator.

Passing Mrs. Garner, Mason stalked after Catarena, but before he could reach her, she'd slipped through the already closing elevator doors. Another vicious curse left his lips along with a promise to turn her ass the most brilliant shade of red at the first opportunity. Two. *I owe you two now, Kitten*, he thought silently.

To his wide-eyed secretary he said, "I want her to personally hand me each and every delivery. You got that, Mrs. Garner?"

Her stern countenance lightened just the slightest bit making Mason squirm, but his secretary said nothing, she just watched him with her knowing eyes. As he passed by her and back into his office, Mason thought he saw her smile.

Chapter Nine

80

Enough was enough, Catarena thought, storming out of the elevator. Walking past a stunned Mrs. Garner, she pushed through Mason's office door and threw the lightweight package at his head. Moving to the side smoothly, he missed the sailing manila envelope without missing a beat in his conversation.

"I'm going to kill you," Catarena thundered, slamming his door closed behind her. All week long, Mason had been using her as his personal mail servant, forcing her to rush up to his office anytime he received any mundane thing. It was getting past the point of ridiculous and Catarena had gone from slightly annoyed to extremely pissed in the span of a few days.

"I'll have someone fax you the cost sheet in a bit," Mason said, talking into the phone. His voice and his words may have been business orientated, but not the sparkle in his deep brown eyes. Mason was amused by her rant, and it only infuriated her further. "Okay. Goodbye."

Mason hung up the phone and looked down disinterestedly at the envelope lying on the floor. Looking up, he leaned back in his black leather chair and rested his hands across his flat stomach, watching her with something akin to humor in his eyes. "When I said I wanted it ASAP, I didn't expect airmail."

Despite her ire, Catarena couldn't help but appreciate his beauty. In a navy blue pinstriped suit, Mason was devastatingly breathtaking, but Catarena wasn't fooled by his looks. No matter how handsome he was, she had to constantly remind herself he was equally as lethal and more than willing to walk right over her to get what he wanted. The only problem was he wanted her.

"I'm not kidding, Mason. I want you to back off."

"What?" he asked, eyes widening in mock shock. "You wanted to keep things just business. I'm obliging you. This so happens to be a very important package."

"That you mailed to yourself," Catarena taunted, placing her hands on her full hips. She was many things, but a fool wasn't one of them. It had taken one quick look at the sender address for everything to click in to place. It was the same address her packages had come from, and it meant only one thing. Mason.

"Your job is to deliver my mail. Why does it matter where it comes from?" he questioned coolly.

"Damn it, is the only person you ever think about yourself?" Mason seemed completely unaffected by what she was saying, which increased her rage tenfold. She was beginning to feel consumed — consumed by her anger, consumed by her hunger and consumed by his relentless pursuit of her.

"You're the one who wanted to play it this way, Kitten. Don't get mad at me when you don't like the outcome of the hand you dealt."

"Is everything a fucking game with you? This is my life, not some company you can take over on a whim."

"I assure you I don't consider this a game," Mason declared evenly. He seemed as cool as could be, but Catarena knew it was all a façade.

"How do you think it looks to everyone else, my coming up here all the time? This is getting damn close to harassment." And she wasn't going to put up with it, not from him or from that stupid-ass Stan who seemed to be mocking her at every turn. It was as if he were taking some kind of sick pleasure in handing her a package to deliver to Mason. As if he were in on a joke. It was annoying and condescending as hell.

Mason stood up as smooth as flowing water and crossed the room in an easy stride. Even with the threat of a lawsuit looming over his head, he still managed to appear unruffled. If she hadn't seen his fervent temper in person, Catarena would have had a hard time believing he was an emotional person, because his icy demeanor was nothing compared to his fiery passion.

"No, Kitten, I believe it is harassment. I could recommend a few good lawyers if you want."

Shaking her head in disbelief, Catarena watched him in awe. He was just so fucking cocky. "You just don't quit, do you?"

"Not when it's something I want." Moving in close to her, Mason walked her backwards until Catarena's back was against the door.

All week long, he had been good, not pushing her at all, but just as she was coming to the end of her rope, he must have been also. His presence, despite her best attempt, was overpowering, and Catarena had a hard time not giving in to him. It was hard to fight him and herself, especially when she just wanted to cave in and let him devour her. She was just as confused as he was controlling.

"You can't have me," she denied, pushing her hands against his hard chest, trying to shove some space between them.

Mason just smiled at her attempt and placed his hands on opposite sides of her head. Leaning down, he whispered against her lips, "Don't you mean again."

"What?" Catarena turned her head, refusing to surrender to him. "Can't find someone in your tax bracket to play naughty games with you?"

"If money is your only issue, Kitten, then you're going to have to think long and hard for something else to use against me."

Ducking under his arm, Catarena moved quickly away from him and farther into his office. Instead of following her as she'd thought he would, Mason simply turned to face her and smiled. The bastard was blocking her only exit. He had every reason to smile.

"It's not the only reason, but it's a big one." Why was she the only one who saw it as an issue? Catarena ran her hand through her shortened locks and let out a frustrated sigh. "Can't we just pretend like it never happened?"

"Can you?" he asked, all humor gone from his face. "I can't get the image of you pleasuring yourself while I watched or the sounds you whimpered when you came out of my head. I can't forget the way you felt beneath me."

Okay, so much for that idea, she thought, wetting her dry lips with her tongue. "Maybe you should have been the writer," Catarena joked, her nervousness outweighing her anger. It was hard trying to stay mad when she couldn't get the image of his words out of her head. "I can't deny it was good—"

"Great."

Sighing, she nodded her head in agreement. This wasn't any easier for her than it was for him but, unlike Mason, Catarena knew how foolish it really was. Despite their immense attraction, they just didn't fit. She knew it, why didn't he? "Okay, great, but nevertheless, Mason, it's just not going to work."

"You keep saying that like it's an option." Mason crossed the room and took Catarena's hand in his, placing it on his bulging erection. "I've been this way ever since you walked into this office. You're not an option for me, Kitten. You're a must."

Catarena's hand tightened around him automatically, her body was willing to accept what her mind just wouldn't. She wanted to deny the equal effect he had on her, but she couldn't. The week hadn't cured her ardor. Her desire for Mason hadn't lessoned, only intensified. "I don't think this is a good idea."

"Stop thinking," he replied, taking her mouth under his in a punishing, passionate kiss. Mason's tongue pushed through her protesting lips and stroked against her own as he pulled her in tighter against his hard, unyielding body.

Catarena's mind clouded with confusion as her body succumbed to his embrace. Wrapping her arms around his shoulders, she moved with him, indulging in his taste like a fine wine. It was hard to push him away when everything inside her craved his touch.

Mason didn't mind the fight in her. The thrill of the chase made his blood boil with arousal. His cock was so hard for her he thought he might burst. As much as he enjoyed her spirit and the fight in her, he also loved the way her body was pressed tightly against him.

The feel of her breasts flattened against his chest, the slight swell of her belly caressing the length of his rigid cock as her warm tongue dueled with his. It was almost enough to make a man forget the punishment he meant to deliver.

Almost.

Mason gathered her impossibly closer, feeling every inch of her curvaceous body glued tightly to his, he then began moving them as one toward the couch lining the far wall of his office.

He settled them on the piece of furniture, loving the way her eyes appeared glossed over, her arousal winning the battle between stubbornness and the need to be touched. "How careful do we have to be?" Mason asked, looking down into her upturned face.

"What do you mean?"

"Are you pregnant or is it still too soon to know?"

Blushing, Catarena shook her head. "No, everything came right on time."

"Great," Yet Mason didn't feel great. The image of Catarena heavy with his child had played a part in many of his most recent dreams.

"I'll be right back, baby," he whispered the words against her ear then licked the lobe, making her shiver.

Mason walked to the door and locked it, keeping his eye on Catarena the entire time. He then went to his desk and, pressing the intercom button, he told Mrs. Garner she was excused for lunch.

At that point, he was expecting some type of argument from his Kitten but she said nothing. Instead, she watched him with her brilliant blue eyes, heavy-lidded with arousal. Soon she would be aroused in a whole new way.

Mason made his way back to where Catarena was reclining on the couch. Sitting beside her, he let his hands wander, up the long expanse of her legs, under her skirt to rest on her inner thigh. Fiddling with the elastic leg of her panties made her shift until her legs were slightly parted. It was an obvious invitation, one Mason didn't plan to pass up, but he also wasn't ready to accept just yet.

"Come here, Kitten," he said, pulling her to her feet until she stood at his side.

"Mason."

The single word was a breathless whisper making him ache. One of these days, he was going to make love to her slow and sweet—in a bed—but it didn't seem such a luxury was in the cards for them just yet.

Today she would learn firsthand what it was like to be punished by a lover, and then when they were both so hot there was no holding back, she would learn what it felt like to be taken.

Mason pulled her close before lowering her skirt. The elastic waist slipped easily over the curve of her hips and was soon pooled at her feet on the floor. Wrapping his arms around her waist, he inhaled her womanly scent then planted an openmouthed kiss just below her navel, before upending her over his lap.

Her shriek of surprise was cut short by the palm of his hand on her ass.

"Don't you dare!"

The twin globes of her ass shimmered nicely beneath the thin silk of her panties.

"Oh, I dare, baby. You have no idea how much I dare."

Mason held her to him with the flat of a hand on her back while he used his other to lower her panties until her ass was bare. His shaft pulsed at the sight of her creamy flesh then dripped proof of his arousal as he ran a finger down the cleft of her ass.

"Have you used the plug I sent?" When she didn't answer he swatted her. "Have you used it, Kitten?"

She was shaking her head wildly, the hair hanging over her face, swaying with the movement. "No."

"We'll have to take care of that real soon, baby, because I mean to take you here too." Mason said the words as he pressed a finger to her rear entrance, teasing, torturing.

Her throaty moan told a story all on its own. The dampness between her thighs heightened his awareness and for the first time since his teenage years, Mason felt as if he were spinning out of control.

Smack!

"This is for cutting your hair," he said as his hand rained down on her upturned ass.

Whack! Smack!

Catarena gasped at the contact, wiggling her bottom over his lap but not as a means of escape. Mason gave her a breather. Slipping his hand between her clenched thighs, he slid a finger into her dripping slit then grazed her sensitive clit. His Kitten was a natural, she arched back trying to take him deeper, to bring herself to completion.

Mason made tsking noises at her antics. "Not yet, Kitten, I'm not done." He finished the sentence with another stinging swat to her now pink cheeks. "And this is for not waiting for me to pick you up."

The next several swats increased in intensity, causing Catarena to pant and squirm. The way she thrust her gorgeous hips with each blow caused Mason's cock to leak pre-come, begging for attention.

When he was finished, Mason ran his hands over Catarena's curves, loving the warmth his hand had put there.

"Time to get up now, baby."

She seemed dazed. Her face was flushed, her peaked nipples pressed against the thin material of her blouse. Mason helped her to her feet and then down to her knees where he was able to kiss her mouth.

He kept the kiss slow and deep, tasting every inch of her warm depths. Palming her breasts, Mason plucked her nipples then rolled them enticingly between his fingers. When she was squirming to get closer, he unbuttoned her blouse, all the while saying silent thanks for her preference of flowing skirts and button-up tops.

When her fingers began fumbling with his belt, Mason leaned back to give her better access. He watched her trembling fingers as she unfastened first his belt and then his slacks. The way she slowly lowered the zipper, as if she were teasing, made his eyes snap to hers. They were bright with arousal and glittering with mischief.

Mason grasped her wrist to stop her. "Be real sure, baby," he warned. Catarena licked her lips in response then freed his raging erection from the confines of his clothing.

"Oh, hell," he groaned. The feel of her delicate hands on his overheated flesh sent a jolt right through his body.

When she lowered her mouth to him, he thought he'd come on the spot. The first swipe of her tongue almost sent him over. Mason gritted his teeth, locking his jaw against the exquisite torture she had thrust upon him.

It took him a moment of total concentration to gather his thoughts. He couldn't allow her to take over. Not this time, not so soon after her first spanking. If he did, she would be hell to live with. Mason grinned at the thought.

Winding his hands through her hair, he held her still. Her eyes flashed blue lasers as they narrowed on him. She was on her knees between his spread thighs, her pink lips wrapped tightly around his cock, and he was stopping her. For a minute, Mason wondered if he'd lost his damned mind.

He locked gazes with her. "My way, Kitten." He said the words as he coaxed her head forward.

Surprise flowed over him when she didn't try to argue or, worse yet, bite. Even though he set the pace, Catarena's talented tongue continued to torture. Mason knew if he didn't stop soon, he'd be lost.

With a sigh of regret, he lifted her mouth from his shaft then kissed her long and hard. He reached into his pocket then handed Catarena the square foil packet he'd come out with.

"Put it on me, baby. I've got to have you now," Mason said, scooting to the edge of the couch to allow for better access.

The sight and feel of her pale hands rolling the barrier protection over his length was more erotic than words. When he was covered, he helped Catarena back to her feet and out of her panties.

She was completely nude from the waist down — and from the waist up, her blouse hung open, nothing more than twin triangles of lace covered her breasts. The erect nubs of her nipples pressed against her bra making Mason's mouth water with the need to taste her.

He urged her forward until she was straddling him on the couch then flicked the front clasp of her bra open. His body was wound so tight he thought he might go off before he had the chance to feel the tight clasp of her pussy around his length.

Mason took her nipple between his lips then sucked strongly. He rolled the other, loving every whimper, every gasping breath she took as he tortured her. His erect cock was at her entrance, but his tight hold around her waist wouldn't allow for much movement.

Her hands were in his hair, tugging him closer to her breasts, her voice pleading as she chanted his name over and over.

He let her nipple go with a plop. "Tell me, Kitten."

"I need to come, Mason. Oh… Oh," she moaned as he moved his mouth to the turgid peak of her other nipple. She was so beautifully aroused, Mason couldn't help the overwhelming desire coursing through his body.

There was no more time to tease. If he didn't give in now, he'd end up making the mind-numbing journey all by himself. With an arm around her waist, Mason lowered his Kitten onto his rigid length, thrusting up at the same time, burying himself hilt-deep in one powerful thrust.

The single, swift motion was all it took to send her into oblivion. Her keening cry of release filled his office, her internal muscles clenched and unclenched as spasm after spasm rocked her body.

Mason held tight, not moving an inch. He wasn't ready to join her just yet.

When he rocked into her, she gasped. "No more, Mason. I can't." Her body shivered with his movement.

"Yeah, Kitten, you can. Again and again until you're hoarse from screaming my name."

Chapter Ten

ဆ

She was going to die. It just wasn't possible to have this much pleasure and survive. Pumping up and down on Mason's ridged length, Catarena had to hold onto his tense shoulders to keep up her pace. Her thighs were quivering and she was milking him for all she was worth, but it still wasn't enough. Mason kept demanding more.

"Give it to me, Kitten," he growled, his fingers biting down into her plump, tender cheeks, forcing her to take more of his cock.

It almost felt like it was too much. Her body was like a spiral of emotions as Mason drove into her over and over again. His thick, hard cock ripped through her as her body pulsed around him trying to accommodate his length. It was painful, it was pleasurable—it was all those things and more.

The more Mason pushed, the more inflamed she felt. They were like combating forces both seeking the same means. "I can't...please...Mason," she begged.

"You can, Kitten," he growled, not giving in to her. Mason tilted her hips, angling his thrust up, knocking against her clit as he powered into her. "Take more of me."

Catarena was sure he was trying to drive her crazy. Her body felt as though it were going to implode from all the pleasure coursing through her system, and just when she thought she couldn't take another second of his loving, she slipped over the edge of reason and came soaring to her peak, screaming his name.

"Take more, more..." urged Mason pumping up into her. Gripping her tightly, Mason roared his release as he brought her down heavily onto him. He held her, not allowing her to move, pumping up into her, wrenching every last drop from his cock.

Catarena trembled as she leaned forward, resting her head against his shoulder, too tired to even sit up to dislodge him from her. Her heart pounded in her chest, beating against her breast as she tried to get her breathing back under control. There was no doubt about it. Mason was incredible. Never had she felt so devoured by someone in her entire life.

After several minutes of only their harsh breathing speaking for them, Catarena pulled up from his pounding chest and asked, "Did I mention this will never work?"

Mason chuckled, causing Catarena to softly groan—she could feel the vibration of his laughter where they were still connected. His cock pulsed inside her, pushing against her tender walls. Smiling she clenched around him, causing them both to groan. She was so deliciously sore. "Yeah, I think you did, a time or two."

"Okay, just making sure I put the warning out there." Easing up, Catarena put her hand between their bodies and grasped the slick-covered condom, holding it down against him as she eased off. At least this time one of them had had the good sense to use protection. She moved down next to him on the lush couch and winced as she sat on her tender bottom. "I should kill you for spanking me."

"If you didn't enjoy it so much, I would say you had a good reason to, but since you did, I'll just say you're welcome," Mason said, standing up. "I'll be right back." He slipped into his bathroom.

Catarena smiled and shook her head. Cocky bastard. Getting up, she pulled on her skirt before she followed him to the bathroom.

"This really can't happen again—"

Mason growled and turned to her. All look of amusement and contentment was erased from her face. "At work, Mason," she continued. She could chalk up the first time to chance, but even she would have to admit there was something going on beyond her control—or better yet—beyond anything she wanted to control. "I've been up here way too long. People are going to start to talk."

"Fuck people."

Catarena rolled her eyes as she fully entered the restroom and took the hand towel he handed her. "I'm not trying to pick an argument with you, I'm just stating facts. Not here again."

Mason turned off his sink and spun Catarena around, pressing her back to the sink. Taking the soapy towel out of her hand, he causally tossed it on the counter and gripped both her hands behind her back in one of his. "I don't think you quite have this whole control thing figured out, Kitten. You don't get to call the shots. I do."

Catarena knew she should have kicked him because of his comment. She was a bra-burning liberal woman who normally in her day-to-day life would never have taken crap from anyone but, for some strange reason, when Mason said Neanderthal things, she wanted to fuck him not club him. "Not here, Mason," she repeated, trying to keep her voice firm.

She wasn't going to give in to him. No matter how much she wanted to. The man was just too damn good for her peace of mind. Even now when she was battling between killing him and kissing him, she couldn't help but quiver just a bit in his presence, and she was beginning to think it had more to do with him—with caring for him—than she wanted to admit, even to herself.

"Let's compromise." Mason released his grip on her wrists, picked her up and sat her on his bathroom counter. The skirt rose up her thighs as he spread her legs and took the cooling cloth off the marble counter, laying it against her tender flesh. He eased the towel between her slightly puffy lips and washed her gently before dipping the towel back into the cold water gathering in the sink. "We'll hold off on the loving during office hours but when you clock out, you're all mine."

His thumb brushed against her engorged clit as Mason began to tease her. Quickly bringing the moisture he had just cleaned away flowing right back again. The arousal blaring in his eyes as he pleasured her told Catarena he received as much out of pleasing her as he did out of fucking her. Alternating between his fingers and the cold towel, he quickly brought her back to the brink, forcing her to hump up onto his hand, fucking herself on his fingers. "Because I won't go a day without this. When you punch out, your day job ends and your night one with me begins."

Arching up, Catarena came for the third time screaming his name. This man was un-fucking-believable, she thought, biting down on her bottom lip, trying to contain the last bit of dignity she had. Mason slipped his fingers out of her sopping center and replaced his probing fingers with the cool towel, shocking Catarena's system, cooling and heating her up all at once.

"Fuck," she groaned as the chilly towel teased her clit. "No more, please."

Mason chuckled as he dropped the towel and began to stroke her hair lovingly. "I do so love the word 'please' on your lips."

"Asshole," she bit out, riding the aftershocks coursing through her body.

A full belly laugh rumbled from Mason, causing Catarena to look up in wonder. For some reason she was willing to bet he didn't do that often. He was too used to being in control of everything from his company to his love life to let loose, and Catarena wanted him to let loose with her. She wanted him to feel as free with her as she did with him.

Smiling, she eased off the counter and slowly got her bearings. It was just too much to take in in one day. She had originally come up to his office to have it out with him — instead they end up fucking again. His office was officially off-limits for her as far as she was concerned. There must be something about an Italian marble desk that worked for her every time.

Yeah, it was the desk and nothing more. Surely not the handsome, heart-stopping, pulse-racing man behind the desk. Maybe if she said that enough times she might begin to believe it, because if she didn't, Catarena would be forced to deal with other things concerning him, like her feelings, which she so didn't want to have for him. If she kept it at just sex, maybe she could survive.

Sighing, Catarena looked at the clock on the wall. She'd been up there much longer than she should have. Catarena just knew Stan was going to have something to say about the time, the slimy little goat. "I have to get back down there."

"You might need these." Picking her panties up off the floor, Mason held them out in front of himself like a trophy. "Although, I am tempted to keep them with me all day."

"Do you really want me walking around here, bending over, picking up packages in this skirt without those?" Catarena asked, raising a brow. She didn't doubt for one second his caveman mentality would cross over into the possessive category.

"Hell, no," he frowned, handing them back to her. Mason sat down in his chair and watched Catarena finish dressing. "What are your plans for this evening?" he asked, picking up a PDA. "We should try to get together for dinner."

"I can't," Catarena said, pushing her skirt down. "I already have plans."

Anyone would have thought she'd said she was walking the boulevard from the way he looked up at her. "Doing what?"

"Not that it's any of your business," she said, looking at him amusedly. "But I'm visiting a club for research tonight."

"What kind of club?" he questioned coolly, setting down the small handheld device.

"A bondage club, of course."

Mason's first thought was, *I am not Job and my patience is gone.* The first thing to come out of his mouth, however, was "No."

"I'm not asking, Mason. I'm going. What I wanted to know is if you would like to join me?"

A growl rumbled up from his chest. "Dammit, Kitten, you don't belong at a bondage club!"

Mason wanted to shake her when she laughed at him. "Calm down, already. I never said I was going to become a gold-card club member, I said I was going tonight and I am—for research."

Her chin jutted out a notch, proving her stubbornness, and Mason wasn't sure whether he wanted to kiss her or spank her again. In the end, he decided to give in. Hell, it was getting to the point where he'd do just about anything to make her flash her beautifully brilliant smile at him, even take her to a bondage club.

"We'll go, but you'll stay by me the whole time."

Catarena looked at him as if he'd grown horns or something. "Let's get some things straight here," she said, her hands perched on the swell of her hips. Her foot was tapping a quick-paced staccato. "You are not my father or my husband, I'll go where I want, when I want. You got that, you big bully?"

Mason stood from where he'd been seated behind his desk. Leaning forward, he placed his fists flat on the surface, bringing him within grabbing distance of where Catarena stood opposite him. She stiffened at the look on his face then took a step in retreat.

"What I've *got*," he bit out the word, "is that even though I may not be your father or your husband, I am in charge when it comes to this relationship. Complete control, Kitten." When she opened her mouth, Mason cut her short. "We'll go tonight so you can do your research, but it'll be on my terms."

"What isn't," she mumbled under her breath.

Mason walked around the desk and caught her up by the elbow. Planting a kiss on her forehead, he then leaned down and nipped her bottom lip. "Finally figured it out, did you?"

His Kitten let loose with a low barrage of curse words aimed at everything from his intelligence to his manhood. Mason chuckled as he thought of ways to curb her sharp tongue.

"Meet me here when you're done. I'll drop you at home to dress then pick you up at eight."

He was extremely pleased when she didn't put up a fuss. His Kitten was pulling him in deeper by the minute. If Mason wasn't careful he'd find himself prone at her feet or kissing the ground she walked on. He was falling fast.

The ride to Catarena's house was done in comfortable silence with his Kitten right by his side. When it came time to let her go at the door, it took all of Mason's willpower not to pull her to him and devour her whole.

The ride from Catarena's house to his gave him plenty of time to think. Of course, all he could think about was loving every inch of her luscious body.

Once at his house, Mason showered and readied himself for a night out with Catarena. He wasn't at all sure what he'd gotten himself into.

Dressed in black slacks and a gray sweater, Mason headed toward Catarena's apartment. He purposefully left the stereo in his car low to give him more time to think. His need for Catarena was great. Not only the physical need that seemed to keep him hard and ready, but the emotional need that made him crave her body and soul.

Mason sat in his car for a minute just staring at her apartment building. He needed to get a hold of himself or he might end up jumping his Kitten the minute she answered the door.

When he felt more in control of his body, Mason exited his car and walked to the apartment Catarena shared with her roommate. He knocked on her door, which was immediately answered by the smart-mouthed roommate again.

"Howdy, boss man," she said as she opened the door wider, indicating he should enter.

Mason nodded his head, afraid to say much. It was obvious the woman needed a keeper. If she wasn't careful, he was going to sic Sebastian on her. Mason smiled at the thought.

"You seem to be in a better mood," she said by way of conversation. Mason nodded his head.

"Cat," she yelled up the hall. "The boss man's here." After the roommate made her very loud announcement, she gathered her purse then gave him a toodle-oo finger wave.

"Tell her to lock up, would ya? I probably won't be home until tomorrow." She winked at him then disappeared through the door, closing it behind her.

Mason heard a noise behind him. He turned just as Catarena came out of her room and almost choked. She was wearing skintight black pants either made of or resembling leather and a tiny red top barely covering the important stuff.

The little vixen smiled brightly, her lips were painted red and her eyes outlined, making them look even more wickedly blue. She looked extremely sexy, stunningly so. Mason's cock throbbed to life in agreement.

Although it took every ounce of his willpower, Mason didn't say a single negative, dominant word about her choice of clothes, nor did he jump her and tear them from her body before plunging into her moist depths. So far so good, he thought silently.

It seemed to Mason that most of the day had been spent in his car either alone or with Catarena sitting close but not nearly close enough. He was relieved to finally arrive at their destination where he could touch her at whim.

"So, where did you hear about this place?" Mason asked as they pulled up in front of a large brick building.

The building was nondescript, just like its name, The Boulevard. The outside gave no clue as to what could be happening through the doors.

"I found it while searching the Internet."

"Figures," he grumbled.

"Aww, come on, this is going to be fun."

She was excited, Mason could tell just by the look on her face. Her flushed cheeks and too-wide smile made her resemble a wide-eyed kid in a candy store. Except for the clothes—they were about as far from childish as a person could get.

Mason opened the door for Catarena then helped her through with a possessive hand at the small of her back. Once his eyes adjusted to the dim interior, he could do nothing but watch Catarena's reaction to her first glimpse of a bondage club.

Tables lined the outer perimeter of the room leaving the center open for dancing. People of all ages cluttered the dance floor wearing anything from jeans and T-shirts to what appeared to be latex. Some were almost nude while others sported collars and leashes.

But it was the stage to the side of the room that caught his attention. There was a small woman in the center of it. She was gagged and bound over some type of table with a look of rapture on her face. The man behind her was swatting her ass, alternating between what appeared to be a flogger, a paddle of some sort and his hand. Every once in a while he would stop, allowing her some time to gather herself before he started in on her again.

It took Mason several minutes to clear his head. The sight before him was extremely arousing. Mason now saw not only the differences between himself and those who chose to live the lifestyle, he also now saw the similarities. He liked to dominate his partner just as the Doms who were teasing and arousing their subs in different ways around the room, but he no longer felt the need to do it in a group setting. As a matter of fact, the thought of sharing his Kitten in such a way was enough to make his blood boil. As long as he had anything to say about it, no one else would so much as look at his woman in a seductive manner.

Catarena stood just in front of him, her eyes wide and bright, the tips of her perky breasts all but begging for attention as they pushed against the red fabric of her barely there shirt. She seemed to melt into him as her eyes focused on the other couples around the room. A slight shiver racked her body causing Mason to wonder just how turned-on the view was making her.

He leaned in close until his mouth was at her ear then whispered, "Next time we'll try it that way."

His words seemed to bring her out of her lust-induced stupor. "There won't be a next time, Mason. I'm not into all this, it's for research, remember."

She was clearly agitated and cuter than hell. Mason pulled her back, snaking his arms around her middle as he did so. He then lifted a hand to her breast, cupping the fleshy globe as if weighing it. When he grazed her nipple, she jumped and gasped.

"For some reason I don't believe you, baby. I'm thinking you loved being spanked by me. The feel of my hand heating your ass made you so wet there's no way you can deny it."

Catarena moaned as she rocked her hips back against his partially aroused length. It seemed to take her a minute to realize where they were and what she was doing. "Stop it!" she hissed.

"All right. For now, Kitten, for now."

Mason led them to a deserted table in the far corner. They still had a good view of everything going on — they just weren't in the middle of it. After ordering drinks, Catarena jumped from her chair as if going somewhere. Mason looked at her, arching a brow in question.

"I'm going to dance so I can find someone to talk to," she said, clearly peeved at having to give him an answer.

Mason wasn't big on dancing, at least not to the loud, raucous beat echoing through the room. He preferred a slower pace, one where a man could hold his woman close.

"Just like that, no partner, no nothing, you're going to dance?"

"Uh, yeah," she said, as if he was missing something.

Mason watched her head toward the dance floor knowing damned well she was fair game without him by her side. She didn't carry herself as a dominant would and wore no show of ownership. She'd find herself the center of attention soon enough if he didn't do something to intervene.

Catarena was moving right along with the rest of the crowd, her body swaying to the thunderous beat of the music. It seemed to be a free-for-all. Not many were partnered up. It wasn't long before a man dressed in black took an interest in his Kitten.

"I don't fucking think so," he cursed when the man placed his hand on Catarena's hip. The damned vixen just smiled and danced out of his reach.

Mason strode to the dance floor where he gave the man a look that could singe and pulled Catarena close to him. He wasn't in the mood to dance but if that was what it would take to keep her from getting groped, thus keeping him out of a fight, he'd do it.

"You're asking for trouble by pushing, Kitten."

She glared daggers at him. "I came to research, Mason, so don't you start with me."

The night only went downhill from there. He followed her everywhere she went, even to the ladies' room, which seemed to piss her off to no end. When she started a conversation, he glared at them until the man cowered and left.

Then, the minute he left her alone so he could use the restroom, she took off. Mason had been franticly searching for her until a waiter came with the message saying Catarena had taken a taxi home.

The only thing Mason could think as he made the drive to Catarena's was that his Kitten had some heavy-duty explaining to do. It never even crossed his mind that he'd been a jackass the whole night. She belonged to him and Mason didn't share.

Chapter Eleven

Catarena couldn't remember the last time she had been this angry. Snatching her watch off, she flung it carelessly down on her vanity, too pissed to care if it was damaged. Her night of research and fun had been ruined, and she had been embarrassed beyond belief by Mason's overinflated ego. That damn, stubborn man was going to be the death of her—or him—she should say, with the way he was going.

At first, the little possessive thing had been kind of cute. Despite living in the era of equality and women's rights, there was something extremely sensual about a man wanting to take charge. Maybe it was because they lived in a world of metrosexuals that a real dominating man actually seemed appealing. In a time where women were singing songs about disappearing cowboys, it was nice to meet someone who wanted to take care of her, but Mason was taking it to an entirely different level.

Catarena couldn't help but be happy she hadn't ended up pregnant, because if Mason was this possessive when it was only her, she could only imagine how crazy he would be if she was carrying his child.

Damn it! This was not how she had pictured the night going. For some strange reason she'd thought she might actually get some work done. To think she'd actually bought this outfit with Mason in mind, and the stupid, frigging jerk hadn't said one thing about it. It wasn't as if she needed his words to affirm how good she looked but a "Hey, babe, you look good" would have worked. Catarena walked into the living room and headed straight for the make-do bar. She needed to release some of her tension before she exploded. Opening up the globe she took out the JD and was pouring herself a drink when her front door began to vibrate from the fist banging on it.

"Catarena, open the damn door this instant," Mason roared from the other side.

Oh, she'd open it all right, and then kick his pompous ass all over the place. Slamming the glass down on the coffee table, Catarena stormed over to her front door and wrenched it open. "You have a lot of nerve—"

"What the hell were you thinking?" he interrupted, pushing himself into her apartment and slamming the door behind him. The noise of the cheap door cracking echoed through the silent apartment. "I ought to spank your ass for leaving the club alone."

"I don't know how to break this to you, He-Man, but I've been leaving clubs for seven years without your help or your permission."

"You don't realize the kind of danger you could have been in."

"No—" Catarena pointed her finger at him, jumping in "—you don't know what kind of danger you're in. You had no right to act the way you did tonight. I told you I was going there to do research. Research, Mason. Research involves meeting, talking to and interacting with people. You knew what you were getting into when I invited you."

"Afraid not, Kitten." Mason's eyes glowed fire, angry and dangerous. "I didn't know your research would entail you being pawed by strange men."

"I wasn't being pawed. And even if I was, what business of it is yours?"

Mason grabbed her arm and pulled her closer to him. "Do you need to be reminded again so soon, Kitten, what business it is of mine."

"Get your hands off of me!" she said quietly but steady. The human body consisted of two hundred and six bones and her four brothers had taught her how to break every single one of them. "Despite whatever sex games we play, you are not now or will ever be my Lord and Master. You're not controlling, Mason, you're psychotic."

Mason released her slowly and stepped back. Catarena brought her hand up and rubbed it against her tender arm watching Mason as he fought to get himself under control. Catarena could see the effort it was taking him, to just step back before he did something neither one of them could take back.

"I've been a writer all my life, but this is the first time anything has called to me like this has. Maybe I've tapped into a side of myself I never knew existed. A side that craves the things we do together and the things I've seen and read about, and this is my time to delve into it. I'm going to write this book with or without your help, Mason, because it's important to me."

His hands were at his side, tightly clinched and as he spoke. "There are safer ways," Mason bit out, still not in complete control of his temper.

"I thought I took the safer route by asking you to go with me."

"What man in his right mind would sit back and let his woman shake her ass in a room full of people getting spanked?"

"My man," Catarena replied coolly. "I'm not asking you to understand what I'm doing. I'm telling you to respect my right to do so or else."

"Or else what?" Mason questioned firmly. "I don't respond well to ultimatums, Kitten."

"And I won't be pushed around," she said just as firmly. "You know what your problem is?"

Raising a brow, Mason crossed his arms, looking at Catarena as if she were the one who was being unreasonable. "I only have one?"

Ignoring his comment, Catarena narrowed her eyes in anger. "You are so used to people kissing your ass that you don't know how to act when someone stands up to you. This control thing isn't a sexual issue. It's an infantile issue. I hate to break this to you, Maverick, but you can't get your way all the time."

"Awful big talk coming from someone who was facedown and ass up over my lap earlier today, getting a spanking and enjoying every last minute, I'd like to add."

"Yes, I was. I admit I enjoyed it, but the difference, Mason, is it's not an all-the-time thing for me."

"I told you when we first met I couldn't turn it on and off. This is me, Catarena, all the time. You either get use to it or—"

"Or what?" she asked crossing her arms. "Like you said to me not more than a few seconds ago, I don't respond to well to ultimatums."

"Then we're at a crossroad, Kitten, because I don't see myself changing any time soon, and I'm damn straight not going to give up on you."

"You're saying it as if there's an option. You either back up and give me room, or you back all the way up and get the hell out of my life."

"Not. Going. To. Happen."

It was as if she were talking to a wall, Catarena thought, bewildered. Nothing she was saying was getting through his thick skull. "You just don't get it, do you? Let me put this in words you might understand." Stooping low, she hunched her shoulders and pointed with her finger. "You caveman. Me intelligent woman. You asshole. Me not going to take it anymore."

"I agree we have a problem." Uncrossing his arms, Mason walked to her floral couch and sat down as if he had all the time in the world. "Starting with the fact your sweet ass left the club without me and we can just wrap it up here because if you're asking for me to change something which comes as natural as breathing does for me, then we have a big problem. I can't give up control, Kitten. I don't know how and, to be honest, I don't think I want to know how."

Catarena wasn't falling for it. "Then you'd better learn."

"What?" Mason smirked at her comment. "Do you think you'll be the one to teach me?"

Raising her brow, Catarena replied, "I just might. I'll be right back." Leaving Mason sitting alone on the couch, Catarena went to her bedroom and picked up the latest thing she had been using for research. Entering the living room, she smiled at him with her hand behind her back. "I think it's about time you learn to give up some of your overworked control and try something new for a change."

"What?"

Catarena moved her hand from behind her back and produced her newest toy. A pair of stainless steel handcuffs dangled off her index finger. "I think it's high time you learned how it feels not to be in control."

Not only was she sexy as hell, she was dangerous to boot. Her sassy mouth was always ready for a comeback and just when he thought he had her figured out, she upped and changed. She was full of surprises.

Mason eyed Catarena with trepidation. He wasn't one for giving up control. The thought of being bound, unable to touch her exquisite curves made him break out in a cold sweat. The thought of her taking her frustrations out on his helpless body made him shiver with apprehension. Too bad he couldn't get the message through to his cock, which had been standing at attention since his Kitten had come out brandishing her shiny silver cuffs.

Seeing her angry wasn't so bad, but witnessing the upset in her eyes tore at him. For the first time since he'd met her—held her in his arms—he felt the need to take things slow, to take her higher than she'd ever been.

"Not going to happen," Mason said, his voice soothing.

She eyed him as if she were mulling something over. "Why not?" she asked, instead of throwing the fit of pique he was preparing for.

"It's just not, baby, but I'm willing to compromise. Give me the cuffs."

Catarena took a hasty step back, shaking her head briskly from side to side. The movement of her head had her hair tumbling wildly around her shoulders.

"Give me the cuffs, Kitten." This time he added an edge to his voice although he was sure to keep it low and calm. "Trust me," he added.

"It's not really a matter of trust, Mason, it's a matter of you screwing with my life."

Catarena still held herself back, keeping herself separate from him. Her words snagged his attention just as Mason's mind had begun to wander, taking into consideration all the things he could do to her cuffed body.

"Excuse me?"

"I'm not willing to be with you if you're going to treat me like a thing—a possession—instead of the intelligent woman I am."

Mason couldn't believe his ears. "What in the hell are you talking about," he growled, not liking the loss of control he felt with what he considered to be a warning. "And you have no choice, Catarena. You are with me, and you do belong to me. So don't pretend you didn't enjoy it when I spanked you or took you over my desk."

Mason wasn't done with the barrage of words he had lined up to remind her just how much she'd loved his possession of her body but Catarena cut him short.

"Damn, Mason! It's not always about sex," she said, her hand running over her face as if she'd lost all patience. "It would be stupid of me to pretend what we do together— what you do to me—doesn't make me hotter than hell but *this* conversation has nothing to do with sex."

He was lost, completely and utterly lost. "It doesn't?"

"Oh, hell." Her words were unemotional and now she looked defeated. "No, Mason, it doesn't."

"Then explain it to me, Kitten, I want to understand. Help me understand." He wasn't good at asking for help so the words were hard to get out, but the thought of losing his Kitten was too mind-numbing to consider. He wouldn't allow it to happen.

"I like what we've got going on, what I don't like is when you take control and apply it to the rest of my life. I've been taking care of myself for a while now and although I'm flattered to have a strong man who cares for me, I won't be treated the way you treated me tonight."

She meant it, every word of it, Mason could tell by the tilt of her stubborn chin, the way she held herself rigid and he was angry with himself and her because of it.

"The man had his hands on you." He couldn't seem to get the vision out of his head.

"That's not the point, Mason. The point is you didn't take the time to see if or how I would handle the situation, you just barreled in and took over. Except for in the bedroom, I don't want to be taken over, Mason. Is it so hard for you to see this from my point of view, to understand?"

Mason heard every word she was saying, he even understood where she was coming from. He hated more than anything to see her upset. Angry was okay, upset was not.

"I understand, baby, but I can't promise anything. I'll try damned hard but it's just the way I'm wired. Will the words be enough for you because I don't give them lightly and I won't make promises I might not be able to keep?"

Catarena dropped her chin to her chest. Her hair swung forward covering her face from his sight and for a minute, Mason felt physically ill. When she lifted her head though, there was a smile curving her full lips.

"I'm not expecting perfect but be forewarned, if you get all macho on me again, I'm gonna kick your ass."

Mason chuckled, relieved to have made some headway. He gathered Catarena close, the fierce need to take his time with her, to take things slow, to make her so hot she thought she'd go up in flames spurred him on. Having Catarena's trust was also something he felt he could no longer do without.

Her face seemed to relax a bit at his words but Mason could still see the wariness in her eyes. "Kiss me, Kitten."

Mason wanted to howl at the moon when she settled her mouth over his for a sweet, submissive kiss. When she handed the cuffs over, he gathered her impossibly closer and initiated another kiss. His mouth slanted over her full lips, lasting and teasing.

His tongue stroked and lapped, thrusting lightly into her warm depths before retreating then delving deep for more. He groaned when she nibbled his lower lip. The feel of Catarena's tongue as she moved it beneath his top lip sent heat spiraling south of his belt buckle.

Mason gathered her so close her cheek was pressed to his chest, trapping her within the curve of his body and arms as he angled her head to deepen the kiss. Although his goal was to go slow and take his Kitten to new heights, his inner beast insisted he possess.

"Which way to your bedroom?" he asked, separating himself from her clinging lips.

Catarena looked dazed. Her pupils were dilated, her cheeks flushed. She opened her mouth to answer but nothing came out. Mason chuckled at the look of utter confusion to cross her face.

With a hand on her legs and one behind her back, he swung her into his arms, cradling her close. "Your bedroom, baby," he repeated, trying to juggle her and the cuffs he still held in his hand.

"The end of the hall."

Her words were breathless, her hands restless as they wandered over his chest. When she reached the bottom of his sweater, she lifted just enough to expose his flesh to her touch. Her hands were cool and soft, mush smaller than his. Mason held his breath waiting to see what she'd do next.

When she wrapped her arms around him, beneath his sweater, then snuggled her cheek against his chest, burrowing deep, Mason couldn't help the sigh that escaped his lips.

When Mason reached her room, he lowered Catarena slowly until her feet reached the floor, making sure her body stayed in contact with his. He then started to undress her.

The red, barely there blouse took no time, but the painted-on leather pants were torture.

Her bra was a concoction of frothy lace invented to entice more than cover. Mason made quick work of it, his control hanging on by a mere thread.

To make matters worse, the tiny triangle covering her mound was damp. The even tinier string that seemed to mysteriously vanish between the full globes of her ass damn near had him swallowing his tongue. Mason opted to remove those with his teeth as his hands lingered on her upper thighs.

As his touch became more intimate, her moans and gasps filled the room. When she was completely nude, Mason stood in front of her and slowly began to remove his clothes. As he did so, Mason removed a condom from his wallet and set it on the bed. Her tentative touch aroused him almost beyond his limits until he was finally forced to shoo her hands away and finish himself.

Completely nude, they stood next to Catarena's bed. Mason reached for the cuffs he'd sat on the bedside table upon entering the room, watching his Kitten as he did so. When he reached for her hand, her eyes widened.

"Trust me," he whispered against her mouth.

With steady hands, Mason closed a cuff around Catarena's left wrist making sure it was snug but not too tight. Shock and surprise glittered in her deep blue eyes when he casually closed the second cuff around his right wrist.

"I don't understand," she said, her words were sincere, questioning.

Mason reached his left hand up to caress the smooth, warm skin of her left cheek. "I'm sorry if I hurt you, baby, but I can guarantee it won't be the last time I make you spitting mad."

Catarena listened to his words then lifted her cuffed hand bringing his with it. "But why this?"

Mason thought about his words carefully before he opened his mouth to speak. "I'm not going to give up control, Kitten, you know that. It's not me. But I did say I was willing to compromise and I stand by my word as you've already learned." He took great pleasure in the blush of her cheeks as she remembered the erotic spanking he'd taken great pleasure in administering. "This," he said, entwining the fingers of his cuffed hand with hers, "was the only thing I could think of to show you how serious I am."

As soon as the words left his mouth Mason pulled back the covers of Catarena's bed then tugged her close for another earth-shattering kiss. After breaking the kiss, he lowered her to the bed.

It was one of the hardest things he'd ever done—holding back the way he was—but Mason was bound and determined.

He trailed kisses over her jaw then lower to her neck, loving the way she arched against him. When she tugged at his hair, trying to pull him to her mouth, Mason growled and nipped the tender spot of flesh where her neck and shoulder met.

Mason smiled against the upper swell of Catarena's breasts when she huffed then relaxed under his touch. He brought their bound hands up beside her head then laid his large palm flat upon her much smaller one, pinning her hand to the bed.

"Tell me you want me," he instructed, as he stroked her nipple with the tip of his tongue.

She arched against him, offering herself, her body. "I want you, Mason. Oh…" she gasped when he grazed the sensitive peak with his teeth then drew it deeply into his mouth, suckling, tugging and pulling until she writhed beneath him. Then he started on the other side.

"How much do you want me, Kitten?" he questioned. The need to hear her voice raspy with arousal pushed him for more.

When she brought her free hand up, burying it in his hair, he stopped what he was doing and looked deep into her eyes. He said not a word, just stared and gave an almost invisible shake of his head.

"I'm going to kick your ass," she groaned, moving her hand from his hair to her side where she grasped the sheet in a white-knuckled grip.

"Uh-huh." The sentiment was mumbled against her nipple before he took it deep in his mouth, just as he had the other.

With Catarena's help, Mason sheathed his cock then nudged her legs apart, settling himself in the V he'd just created. He moved until his shaft was perched right at her entrance. "How much, Kitten?"

"You're killing me, Mason. Just fuck me already. Please," she added in haste when he narrowed his eyes at her.

Mason thrust his hips forward stopping when the head of his cock was engulfed in the warmth of her pussy. Catarena raised her hips in hope of drawing him deeper, but Mason was ready.

His Kitten grew frantic beneath him. Her legs were now wrapped tightly around him, urging him closer. "Oh, God. I need you in me. Hurry!"

Her breathy words broke the dam of Mason's control and in one quick thrust, he was buried inside her pulsating sheath. His ears rang and the room spun before he reined in his lust.

Catarena wasn't as ready to take things at an easy pace. Her body writhed and lifted beneath him, coaxing him with its internal heat and overwhelming need.

Mason lifted his free hand then smoothed Catarena's hair from her face. Perspiration dotted the bridge of her nose and her forehead.

"Look at me," Mason commanded. When her eyes snapped open, locking on his, he lowered his mouth to hers, tasting her sweetness, her independence and strength. "Slow down, Kitten."

Catarena was shaking her head before Mason even finished his sentence. "I can't, Mason. Don't make me, not this time."

Mason's full weight on top of her pinned her to the bed with ease. Her legs moved restlessly on each side of him, her body searching for its release. Mason could feel the tiny, pulsing tremors as they coursed up and down the length of her internal muscles.

"Tell me how, Catarena. Tell me how you need it, baby, tell me how you want it."

Mason watched as her teeth snagged her lower lip then quickly released it. It was as if she had no idea what she wanted, what she needed, and then she surprised him once again.

"I want it hard and fast. I need to feel you deep inside me, Mason."

Her words were calmly said, slow and sure. They ignited a heat inside him like nothing he'd ever before experienced.

He thrust deep and hard, picking up the pace when Catarena matched him thrust for thrust. With his hands on the side of her head, Mason held her still for the possession of his mouth. A deep, rumbling groan welled from his chest as he felt her shatter around his length.

The tightness of her sheath milked his cock. Mason could feel every ridge, every ripple as her body grasped his tightly. Her keening cry of release sent him over the edge, the pleasure bordered on pain it was so intense.

Chapter Twelve

ဢ

Life was good, there was no doubt about it. For the first time in a long time Catarena was happy with every aspect of her life. The book was coming along smoothly—thanks to countless hours she and Mason were putting in and the chance meeting she'd had with a real-life Dom—Catarena was pages past her halfway point.

It was an overwhelming feeling of accomplishment to see her dream of writing an erotic novel becoming true. Sometimes she had to pinch herself, because it all seemed too good to be true, but whenever she needed a reality wakeup call all she had to do was roll over and he was there.

Mason, despite her initial misgivings, had really been trying to corral his caveman ways. It wasn't always springtime and puppies, but the good times were definitely outweighing the bad. They were even getting to the point where he growled at her softly instead of blowing his top when she did something he didn't agree with. It may not seem like much to some, but Catarena knew what a big step it was for him, and she was happy he was trying. So happy in fact, she was planning a little surprise for him, even thinking of giving him an award for the most improved, possessive boyfriend. If she knew Mason as well as she thought she did, he was going to love it.

"Back from lunch already?" asked Stan, entering the room where she was sorting the last of her mail. The good mood she had been swimming in instantly dissolved. Stan had that way about him. A genuine fun-sucker if ever there was one.

Refusing to rise to the bait, Catarena continued sorting the envelopes on the counter. "Do you really think it's fair you get a longer lunch break than everyone else, just because you're fucking the boss?" he baited, not detoured by her silence.

Biting back the words trying to escape, Catarena took a deep, calming breath. "I wasn't late back from lunch. If you want to check my timecard, you'll see I clocked in five minutes early."

Catarena and Mason hadn't even had lunch together — ever. It was one of the things she insisted on. She wanted to keep their work relationship as professional as possible, even going as far as convincing him to remove the silly rule about her being the only person to deliver his mail. But, of course, it wasn't good enough for Stan.

"Well, that's today."

"If you have a problem with my work performance or my tardiness, feel free to take it up with the powers-that-be."

Snorting, Stan gave an evil look. "Do I look stupid to you?"

"Do you want me to answer you?" So much for playing Ms. Nice Guy. Catarena was damned tired of putting up with his snide comments.

"You better watch how you talk to me, missy. I don't care who you're sleeping with, I'll can your ass."

"No, Stan." Catarena turned to face him, annoyed rather than mad. He was just a pitiful little man who took out his rotten existence on everyone around him. "You better be careful who you're talking to."

"What? You going to take it up with your sugar daddy?" he sneered.

"No, I'm going to take it up with personnel and file a sexual harassment complaint. I don't have to take this from you."

"Who do you think they will believe?"

"I don't know, but I'm willing to find out. Are you?"

Stan's eye twitched as his hand shot out and grabbed her arm. Catarena was shocked by the fact he'd dare touch her. Stan had tried to intimidate her, but this was the first time he'd ever dared to touch her. "Dolls like you come and go, but when he's tired of you, who will you have left in your corner?"

"She'll have me," Bailey said, startling Stan into dropping his hand from her arm. Crossing the room, Bailey walked over to Catarena's side and stood next to her friend showing a united front. "You know, Satan, for a man who thinks he so smart you're constantly making stupid decisions."

"What, picking on your friend?"

"No harassing her with your back to the door and the door wide open—that was stupid, but the thing that makes you king of all idiots, is not only the fact that you dared to touch her but you're berating someone who you allege is sleeping with the boss. How stupid are you? If she is fucking him, no matter how long their relationship is destined to last, he will, by nature, side with her and do anything and everything he can to keep in her good graces." Raising a perfectly sculpted brow, she finished. "Including firing your ass."

"You better watch it, Ms. Edwards," he warned, turning his anger from Catarena to Bailey.

"No you better watch it," Catarena spoke up. She didn't want to chance Bailey being fired for sticking up for her. "Back off or I'll report you. I'm not kidding."

Stan didn't comment, just watched them for a second before he turned and stormed out of the room. Catarena sighed and let out a breath she hadn't known she had been holding. She wasn't one for confrontations, but she also wasn't the type of person who let someone bully her. For some reason she seriously doubted Stan was just going to back off. He gave off a negative energy, which made her shiver with trepidation.

"Woo, that was fun." Bailey bumped hips with her and smiled. "We haven't tag-teamed on people in years. Ooohh, I've got an idea, let's go attack that bitch Betty. I know she drank my soda."

"Bailey…"

"What?" she asked frowning. "I had my name on it and everything."

"Not that." Despite herself, Catarena couldn't help but smile. "I'm talking about Stan. You shouldn't have interfered."

"Yeah, right, like I was just going to sit there and let him talk mad trash about you. I don't think so."

"You could get fired."

"And he could kiss my black ass. This is a job, honey, not a career. I've got a little less than a year before I'm done with school. Then I'm just going to walk around telling people way off, starting with that weasel."

"Still…" Bailey might act indestructible, but she wasn't, and Catarena would feel horrible if anything happened to her.

"Still nothing. Besides you *are* doing the boss. The least you could do is get some perks, I mean besides the obvious, of course." Bailey wiggled her eyebrows suggestively, forcing Catarena to laugh. "On a serious note though, I think you need to let him know what Satan is doing."

"No," Catarena stated firmly. "I don't need Mason intervening on my behalf. He is controlling enough, one word about this and he'll pack me up in an ivory box and kill Stan."

Tilting her head to the side, Bailey acted as if she were contemplating the idea. "I don't know, the killing Stan part might be worth it."

"Not to me, thank you very much." Catarena had barely gotten Mason to chill out, and she just knew—she just felt from the bottom of her soul—Mason would go all commando and insist on solving her problem for her.

With her loaded cart in tow, Catarena and Bailey walked out of the mailroom together. Heading toward the elevator, she passed a glaring Stan who was standing in his office doorway watching them. Catarena turned her head, refusing to even look at him. If at all possible, she wanted as little contact with him as feasible. Something about him just wasn't right. Stan was the type of person who preyed upon people he considered weaker than him. If she let him walk over her, he would continue moving on from person to person. It had to stop somewhere.

Catarena had several hours before she could go home and she wanted to spend them as stress free as possible. Taking the elevator up to the top, she cheered up a bit. She hadn't seen Mason since the day before. They'd both been rather busy the last couple of days and hadn't been able to mesh their schedules together. Which was a bit of a sore point with Mason because he didn't understand why Catarena didn't just move in with him.

Despite the fact they had only been together for less than two months, Mason was already gung-ho about her moving in and although the idea did seem appealing to Catarena, she was still very hesitant. Part of her was afraid Mason would just consume her whole if she did, and the other part wasn't so sure how she would fit into his world. Even now, she insisted on him coming to her place instead of her going to his.

She had only been to his house once before and it was hard for her to imagine living there. Cold and beautiful, it reminded her of an art exhibit. She could look all she wanted but she dare not touch for fear of breaking something. All the raises in the world wouldn't pay to replace a vase in his house if she broke it.

Smiling at Mrs. Garner, she parked the cart out of the way and knocked softly on Mason's office door.

"Come in," he bellowed from within.

Opening the door, Catarena paused as she stood in the threshold. Mason never failed to take her breath away. Handsome and debonair, he was definitely a sight for sore eyes. Looking up, he smiled, and for the first time ever, Catarena finally understood what love felt like. Her chest expanded and her heart opened, and she just wanted to smother him with her joy. It was more scary than wonderful and entirely too real.

Catarena felt frozen in her tracks. What was she suppose to say to a man she'd just realized she loved? The only thing that came to mind was, "Hi."

The look on Catarena's face made Mason's heart beat double-time. She looked as if the air had been knocked out of her in a good way.

"Hi," he answered back, recognizing the huskiness of his own voice.

Mason stood and slowly moved around his desk. He held an arm out then inhaled deeply of Catarena's glorious scent when she fell into his arms. Their kiss was deep, heated and slow. Mason took them to new heights then moaned deep in his throat when his Kitten matched the thrust of his tongue with her own.

"Have dinner with me tonight?" Mason asked when he finally broke the kiss. He gave his best shot at keeping his voice neutral. He wanted it to be an invitation, but it more than likely came out a command.

Catarena had been busy the past couple days and although it had almost killed him, he was trying to understand. Not an easy thing to accomplish when his mind insisted he drag her home—to his home. His cock stood at attention every time the thought of her so much as passed through his mind, which just happened to be all the time.

Needless to say, Mason had spent the past couple of days not only frustrated, but hard and frustrated. "Okay," she answered, her blue eyes glittering with emotion. "Where did you want to go?"

"I made reservations for the new Italian place up the street."

She smacked him lightly with the flat of her hand on his chest. "Pretty sure of yourself, aren't you?"

Catarena said the words with a smile but Mason had the feeling she wasn't kidding.

"It's my turn to pick, Kitten, and if I hadn't made the reservations early, we wouldn't have a seat."

Her eyes darted away briefly before settling back on him. "I'm not very comfortable with going to a fancy restaurant, Mason. It's not really my type of place."

"You'll be fine, baby," Mason soothed, not liking the doubt in her beautiful blue eyes. It bothered him how she didn't want to share in that part of his life. "Is there anything I can do to make it more comfortable for you?"

Catarena stepped away from him then turned to pace the length of the room and back. Her eyes were squinted in concentration, making her look absolutely adorable. On her way back, her gaze snapped to his and another of her world-famous smiles curved her mouth.

"Can Bailey come?"

The question took him by surprise but Mason hid it well. "Sure, Kitten, whatever you want."

She brought a finger to her lips, pondering another mystery of life, if the look in her eyes was any indication.

"Is there a friend you can bring too? We can make it a double date."

Mason didn't have to give her question much thought. He had the perfect man in mind to turn loose on her feisty roommate. "Yeah, I've got a friend who would enjoy a night out with a woman as beautiful as Ms. Edwards."

Catarena eyed him speculatively as if she could see inside his head and knew wicked thoughts were churning in there. The wheels were already spinning and Mason couldn't help but be curious about how Sebastian and Bailey would deal with each other.

"Back to work, Kitten. I'll be waiting for you when you get off."

She raised herself up on her toes and pecked his cheek, acting as if the small gesture was going to be enough.

"I don't think so," he mock growled, pulling her flush against the length of his body before lowering his head to kiss her senseless. Mason's breathing was still accelerated when she strolled out the door of his office.

It was hard to get back to work after feeling her breasts against his chest. The restless movement of her legs against the thigh he'd wedged between hers had him hard and ready in no time. Even now, he was having a hard time keeping his libido in check. He wanted nothing more than to call her back to his office and fuck her until she screamed his name over and over.

Catarena met him at his office. She never ceased to amaze him. Thinking back, Mason was absolutely positive Catarena was the only one who had ever made his stuffy secretary Mrs. Garner smile. The little imp could probably charm the Pope out of his boxers.

He thought about his Kitten even after he dropped her off at home. It bothered him that she wouldn't move in with him but Mason didn't push. They were still very early in their relationship, which hadn't started out normally to begin with.

What really irked him was the fact she hadn't yet spent so much as a single night at his house. Mason couldn't figure out why and he hadn't asked, not wanting to start a fight. He wasn't yet ready to admit to himself, or anyone else, how his feelings were just as involved as he guessed Catarena's were.

The vision of her beneath him in the large expanse of his king-size bed had kept him awake many nights. Mason wanted nothing more than to hold her naked body against his throughout the night knowing full well she would be there the following morning.

For the first time in his life, Mason didn't shudder at the thought of marriage. It was scary how fast it had happened. How quickly the thought of a wife and kids had snuck up on him.

That's because you love her, you idiot, the little voice in his head shouted.

Love? Could it be? The single question played over and over in his mind as he dressed for dinner. Mason shook away the thought. He'd think about it later when he had more time to mull over the emotions bound and determined to drive him crazy.

He'd called Sebastian before lunch, inviting him along for the fun. Mason didn't know much about Catarena's roommate Bailey, but he did know Sebastian, and tonight could prove to be very interesting.

Mason picked Catarena and Bailey up at their apartment. He had a hell of a time keeping his hands off his Kitten. The black cocktail dress she'd chosen for the night hugged her curves as snug as a glove and if Mason's eyesight wasn't failing him, he would swear there were no panty lines beneath it. He couldn't wait to run his hands down the swell of her ass to find out firsthand what, if any, panties she was wearing beneath the barely there strappy dress.

"Keep devouring her with your eyes like that, boss man, and I'm going to feel like a third wheel here." The words were whispered low, for his ears only as they entered the restaurant.

The lighting was low, casting sexy shadows over Catarena's bare shoulders. The low murmur of voice could be heard from the other room along with the clink of crystal and silver. It was one of the best restaurants in town, which was why Mason had chosen it. His Kitten deserved only the best.

"I'll be right back." Catarena said the words against his cheek before leaving him and Bailey alone.

Mason pulled his gaze away from the gentle sway of Catarena's hips as she headed for the ladies' room. He turned to Bailey, a smile on his face.

"Bailey, I told you to call me Mason. And you won't be a third wheel because Sebastian should be here any minute."

Bailey gave her head a saucy shake then winked at him. "Whatever you say."

Mason had just opened his mouth to scold Bailey when Catarena came back into the room, her dress flowing softly around her knees. He was so busy watching her, he missed Sebastian entering through the front door.

Mason made introductions then alerted the hostess they were ready to be seated. The four of them were shown to a quiet corner. The cozy booth was bathed in candlelight giving it a romantic ambiance.

Catarena and Bailey slid into the booth. Mason followed his Kitten, quickly pulling her close so they were touching thigh to thigh.

Sebastian followed Bailey, they were talking low between themselves and Bailey had a wicked little smile on her face. Mason wondered if Bailey would automatically think that due to his staid business suit, wire-rimmed glasses and easygoing manner Sebastian was the type of man a woman could easily manipulate. He wasn't, but Mason didn't feel it was up to him to warn the impudent vixen that Sebastian took his bedroom play even more seriously than Mason himself did. She'd have to find out all on her own.

Mason ran his hand along Catarena's thigh down to her knee and then back up, taking the length of her dress with it. When his hand touched warm, soft skin, he couldn't help but sigh with contentment.

His Kitten, who was trying to act as if nothing was happening, asked Sebastian, "So, how did you and Mason meet?"

He could feel the quivering muscles of her thigh as his fingers inched closer to her sex. When she clamped her thighs closed, he chuckled.

"Not here," she hissed as he leaned into her.

He stroked the curve of her neck with the tip of his tongue causing her to shudder slightly. "Party pooper."

Chapter Thirteen

೫

Going commando to a restaurant with a butt plug stretching and filling her wasn't the smartest thing Catarena had ever done. Especially when accompanied by Mason. The man was like an octopus, hands coming out of everywhere, caressing her and driving her damn near insane. If she didn't love it so much, she might complain but, then again, where was the fun in all of that?

Dinner was going much better than she'd anticipated though. Everyone seemed to be having a great time and Catarena was very happy Mason had invited Sebastian along because it had given her a chance to see Mason around his friend. It was strange seeing Mason and Sebastian together. It was almost as if he were a different person. The same controlling workaholic was there, but underneath it was a different side. A more relaxed side.

Sebastian was full of tales from their days at the university, and although Catarena was sure she was getting the PG-13 version, it was still fun to listen to. It allowed her an insight to the man she had come to love, and humanized him in a way she never thought possible. It was, for the lack of a better word—enchanting.

The best part, though, was she wasn't the only one having a good time. Bailey and Mason seemed to be hitting it off rather well, which was great since it was very important to Catarena that the two people she cared the most about got along, and they did, surprisingly well, but Mason wasn't the only one Bailey was charming.

"If you gentleman will excuse me," Bailey said with a smile. Sebastian moved over, allowing Bailey to scoot out of the booth and disappear toward the bathroom. Sebastian turned and looked at Catarena with a slight grin on his face. "I thought you women traveled in pairs."

"Only when we want to complain about our dates." The comment wasn't entirely true, but it was a lot easier to say than "your friend won't keep his hands off my thighs so my skirt is riding up and I'm not wearing any underwear". Not to mention the fact she was so hot and ready that the slightest bit of movement would manipulate the base of the plug filling her and probably have her climaxing at the table for all to see. Once again, Catarena came to the conclusion that wearing a plug while sans panties and accompanied by an octopus wasn't such a brilliant idea.

"Oh, really." Sebastian looked toward the rear of the restaurant where Bailey had disappeared with a quizzical look on his face, before turning his dark green eyes back to Catarena. "So if you were a betting woman, how would you rate my chances with Bailey?"

Catarena didn't want to be rude, but she seriously doubted he was Bailey's type. Bailey was a very attractive woman who never lacked for a date, and although Catarena had seen her go out with many different guys of varying ethnicity, all the men were usually drop-dead gorgeous. It wasn't as if Sebastian was unattractive, he just didn't seem to have the flair Bailey was normally drawn to. "Well, she's actually kind of seeing someone right now—several someones really."

"So no one too serious?"

"Well…" she evaded. Catarena didn't want to lie right out, but she didn't want Sebastian getting his hopes up. "I guess not."

"Great," Sebastian smiled, and for a moment Catarena was drawn into him. He was nowhere near as attractive as Mason was but there was something about him. "How about an insider's tip?"

"Don't ask if you can touch her hair," Catarena kidded. It was a running joke with her and Bailey. One of Bailey's pet peeves when it came to dating people of other races. They could never figure out why people were drawn to Bailey's hair. No matter how she styled it, whether in braids or loose and natural, someone, somewhere would make a comment, and then Catarena would have to step in to rescue the poor soul.

"Is this a common warning you have to give people?" enquired Mason who had somehow, once again, slipped his hand under the table so he could caress her thigh.

Picking up her fork, she pointed it with a warning glare at Mason who chuckled and moved his hand. "People are really weird."

"That's putting it lightly," stated Bailey, standing at the table again. Sebastian moved so she could get in and she sent him a light, flirty smile. "There was a woman in the bathroom."

"Should we call security?" joked Sebastian.

Rolling her eyes, she smiled at him. "I don't know, you're the lawyer, you tell me. Is it illegal to charge for breath mints?"

"I don't believe so."

"The woman was just sitting there with a tray full of stuff which, and I quote, 'You're welcome to use' but then you have to tip her. As if I'm going to tip her for letting me use someone else's lipstick."

What an image, Catarena thought, shuddering. "That's just nasty."

"Who are you telling?"

The women shook their heads in disgust as the men sent each other a knowing smile over their heads. Pushing his glasses back up, Sebastian asked, "So let me ask you ladies a question. Is Mason an ogre to work for?"

"The pits." Winking at Mason, Catarena groaned. "He's such a terrible taskmaster."

"Taskmaster, huh? Is that the nickname you gave him in the BDSM room?" Sebastian commented, forcing Bailey to choke on her glass of wine. Catarena on the other hand wasn't so amused. Turning to Mason who had a "what did I do" look on his face, she elbowed him in the side. "I can't believe you told him."

"Well, I can't believe he repeated it." Narrowing his eyes at Sebastian, Mason continued. "But I'll guarantee you he won't tell anyone else."

"I'm just trying to have a little conversation."

"Pick a new topic," Mason warned.

"Hold up on the new topic. I want to know, how come lawyer boy here seems to know more about what's going on than I do." Setting her glass back on the table, Bailey crossed her arms over her ample breasts.

"There's nothing to tell." Muttering under her breath, Catarena vowed to kill everyone at the table if they didn't shut up.

"Maybe we can compare notes later," Sebastian said, looking over at Bailey. "I'm sure you have some goods you wouldn't mind parting with."

Raising a brow, Bailey smiled at him slowly. "I'm well-equipped with goods."

"So I see. What about you, Bailey?" Sebastian said focusing all of his attention on her. "What do you think of Mason?"

"Well," she drawled out, looking over at Mason. "For some strange reason he seems less imposing now that I hear him groaning in the other room." Sebastian roared with laughter as Mason and Catarena both went a little red in their cheeks. "But he does have crappy taste in supervis—" Bailey let out a loud yelp, jumping in her seat when Catarena kicked her under the table on the ankle.

This was not the time and surely wasn't the place for that conversation. Despite Bailey's persistence, Catarena was still adamant in not telling Mason about Stan. She wanted to deal with it in her own way.

"Are you having a problem with your supervisor?" Mason queried, frowning over at Bailey. Catarena understood something Bailey just didn't quite get. Mason's overprotectiveness was going to extend to her as well. It was just how he worked.

"No, not really," Bailey hedged, shooting Catarena a "help me" look. "He's just not my favorite person."

"If you're having any trouble with him—"

"I'm not." Which wasn't an exact lie, Stan was giving Catarena the hard time not Bailey. "Speaking of trouble though, I was wondering something."

"Yes?" Mason asked, still in a serious mood. He didn't recognize the twinkle in Bailey's eyes the way Catarena did.

"Do you prefer to use a particular hand when you spank?"

This time it was Sebastian who choked on his laughter and wine. Catarena was going to kill her, smite her where she sat if she didn't shut up.

"Bailey, I have a question for you," Mason said, tapping his fingers on the table next to his glass.

"Fire away, boss man."

"Can I touch your hair?"

* * * * *

A couple of hours had passed but Mason still couldn't get the strange conversation out of his mind. It was completely mind-boggling how well Sebastian and Bailey got along. With the same twisted sense of humor, they could almost finish each other's jokes and Mason wasn't even going over the fact that after only a few hours of sitting next to each other at a dinner table, they acted as if they'd known each other for life. It was damned strange.

When Sebastian invited Bailey to a movie, Mason had been a bit worried. Although his friend never seemed to be without female companionship when he appeared to want or need it, Catarena had told him Sebastian wasn't Bailey's type. In fact, he was the complete opposite.

It seemed as if sassy Bailey with the quirky sense of humor lusted after bad boys. Sebastian might not resemble a bad boy on the outside, but inside, he was pure dominant kink. The corner of Mason's mouth lifted in a smile. Didn't the old adage say one should be careful what they wished for?

Mason brought his attention back to the woman sitting quietly in the passenger seat of his car. He already knew the answer but asked the question anyway.

"My place or yours, Kitten?"

She looked at him. For a minute her blue eyes bore into his, a brief flash of discomfort passing over them but all she said in answer was, "Mine is closer."

It wasn't necessarily the truth but Mason wasn't up for a fight, although soon they were going to have to talk things over. Since he'd realized how deep his feelings for Catarena ran and knew beyond a shadow of a doubt she also had at least some feelings for him, he just couldn't allow things to remain as they were. Not if there was any hope of the two of them moving forward in their relationship.

Mason headed toward her house with thoughts of her silky thighs fresh on his mind. He reached his hand, bypassing the gearshift for her thigh. Once again, he trailed his hand down and then back up, taking the skirt of her dress with it.

"You drove me crazy all through dinner," she said, parting her thighs slightly.

Mason walked his fingers over her thigh but never once touched her heat. "Then my plan worked, didn't it, Kitten?"

Catarena dropped her head onto the seatback and licked her lips. Her whispered words made his cock throb uncomfortably behind the zipper of his slacks.

"I have a surprise for you."

He looked at her, silently compelling her to do the same. When she finally turned her head and fluttered her heavy-lidded eyes open, Mason thought he would have to pull over onto the shoulder of the road and take her hard and fast. The thought of driving the few miles it would take to get to her apartment seemed to be too much.

"Tell me, Kitten." His voice was strained, gruff as it filled the interior of his car.

She gave him a smile hot enough to melt metal then shook her head. "You know better than that, Mason. It wouldn't be a surprise then."

"Brat," he accused, more aroused than ever.

Mason thanked the stars when they finally pulled up in front of her apartment building. The short trek from his car to her apartment was riddled with kisses and short groping sessions against whatever smooth surface was large enough to support them.

"Get a room," someone yelled from across the street, bringing Mason temporarily out of his lust-induced insanity.

He cursed a blue streak as he pried his mouth from Catarena's, pulling the top of her dress back up so she was decently covered. Damn, he'd almost exposed her.

"I'm sorry, baby," he said.

Catarena laughed her deep, throaty laugh then fumbled for her keys. When she found them, she grabbed his hand and dashed to the door of her apartment. The woman was absolutely amazing.

They made it through the front door and into the kitchen where Catarena sat her purse on the counter. When she turned, he was there to gather her close, pinning her to his body with his arms.

"I've got to touch you," he groaned against her mouth. "Ever since you walked out in this little number," he said, running a hand down her back to rest on the curve of her ass.

"So touch me," she said the words then nipped his lip playfully. "Let's see if you can figure out what your surprise is."

"Tease."

"No teasing allowed, Mason, not tonight. Tonight, if you find it, it's all yours or you can take a rain check and we can enjoy something else. Entirely your choice."

Mason wasn't sure if he could wait a minute longer. He backed up until the counter was at his back then leaned against it, his legs braced wide. After pulling Catarena into the V of his spread thighs, he proceeded to slowly lower the spaghetti straps of her dress until the bodice was perched on the edge of her erect nipples.

"Breathtaking," he said as his head dipped for a taste.

Catarena arched toward him as if his mouth on her flesh were more important than her next breath. Mason ran his hands over the swell of her ass, gently squeezing the enticing globes.

Catarena gasped lightly as Mason continued to manipulate her body. His hands stopped squeezing and instead his fingers began tracing.

"I wondered if you had anything on under this. It drove me crazy all night long, but you knew it would, didn't you?"

Her smile was bright, the curve of her lips showed off the white of her teeth. The twin dimples bracketing her luscious mouth called to his tongue. Mason, all of a sudden, had an overwhelming urge to taste.

When he leaned in close, dipping his tongue tauntingly into the gentle valley, all the while his hand played with her bottom, she whispered, "You're getting warmer."

Mason lifted his head. He stared deep into her eyes as his hands roamed over the silky fabric of her cloth-covered ass. Bending at the knees, he grasped and lifted her dress until it was bunched around her waist.

"Hold this, Kitten." His words were no-nonsense, intense. Catarena shivered with what he hoped was anticipation. She did as he asked.

When her dress was fully out of the way, Mason leaned back onto the kitchen counter. With his knees bent slightly, he pulled Catarena to him. Grasping both legs at the lower swell of her ass, Mason ground his erect shaft against her. He felt it then.

She was wearing the butt plug he'd bought her. "Fuck," he swore.

"Surprise."

The single word turned in to a gasped moan as Mason brushed the base of the toy lodged firmly within her body.

"You've had this in all night?" he asked, running a finger around the base, adding just enough pressure to get her attention.

His Kitten moaned again, her body quaked against his with each pass of his finger, but other than that, she remained silent.

Mason wanted to pull the toy from her body and replace it with the length of his cock, but it was too soon. He pulled at the base until the width of the plug burned and stretched the tender ring of muscles protecting her.

Catarena gasped, her eyes flying open in a mixture of pain and pleasure. "Answer me, baby. Did you have this in all night?"

"Y-yes," she said, gulping air as Mason gently pushed the toy back into her body.

She expelled the breath she'd been holding, her eyes once again closed. "Is this the first time you've used it?" Mason asked, accompanying the question with a twist of the toy's base.

"Oh! Umm, yes. Yesss!" she hissed against Mason's shoulder when he changed the direction he was rotating the toy.

"Do you have any idea what this does to me, what you do to me?"

His Kitten looked up then licked her dry lips. The tip of her pink tongue peeking out from between her full lips was all it took to send Mason over. Still holding her close, he backed her to the kitchen table. Once there, he lifted Catarena until she was firmly seated on the tabletop.

The contact between her toy-filled ass and the cool surface of the table elicited a gasp of surprise. Mason could imagine how her weight caused the plug to lodge even deeper into her body's heat.

Mason jerked her to the edge of the table needing to taste her more than anything. "Lean back, Kitten. I want full access of your pretty, pink pussy."

He knew his words were considered crude but he was so hungry for her he couldn't think straight. Catarena leaned back on her elbows then spread her thighs wide.

"Good girl," Mason murmured, before he settled his mouth over her slit, taking as much as he possibly could as he thrust his tongue into her, tasting her, teasing her.

He sucked one of her fleshy nether lips into his mouth, loving everything about her. The taste of her essence, the warmth of her flesh against his tongue. He was absolutely lost, a man barely hanging on. Mason knew if he didn't sink his cock into her and soon, he was going to go up in flames. It was as necessary as breathing—his feeling her from within.

The fist tightness of her vagina would burn even hotter due to the fullness caused by the butt plug he'd insist remain exactly where it was. But before he could do as he wanted— as he needed—Mason would send her flying.

With quick flicks of his tongue, Mason tortured Catarena's clit. She was writhing and moaning, calling his name and yet it wasn't enough. Mason wanted more, insisted on more. When he thrust two fingers into her, his Kitten spiraled out of control. Mason urged her on by plunging in and out of her body while nudging the base of the plug, wringing every last sensation from her body.

"It's a good thing I picked out the smallest plug available to start you off with, baby. You're so tight around my fingers I don't know if my cock would have fit with a larger plug filling you."

When she lay limp and still on the table, her quivering internal muscles no longer milking his fingers, Mason lifted her into his arms and headed for her bedroom. He was far from done.

Chapter Fourteen

❧

Mason carried her all the way to her room before lying her down carefully on her bed. He stepped back and turned on the lamp located on her desk, bathing the room in a soft, sensual glow. Easing up into a sitting position, Catarena carefully rolled over until she was on her stomach, alleviating some of the pressure from the plug.

All through dinner, Catarena had been aware of its presence. Whenever she moved, it moved, dancing around in her body, constantly reminding her of what she had planned. She had known Mason would love it, she just hadn't realized how much. He had been an animal feasting on its last meal, and she had loved every second of it.

"I want you on all fours, Kitten," Mason commanded as he began to undress.

"What's the magic word?" Catarena teased, easing up onto her knees. Kneeling on her bed, she watched Mason's face cloud over a bit, his teeth bared as he dropped his shirt to the ground. His need for her was as apparent as the thickening air in the room.

"Now," he growled, moving his hand slowly to his belt buckle. Pulling the leather slowly out of the buckle, he tapped his finger against the strap, before leisurely pulling it out of the loops. "Or do I have to tell you twice?"

Catarena felt bold and alive at that moment. Never before had she been so sure of her own sexual power as she was at that instant. The fact she could make Mason want her so much was like an aphrodisiac coursing through her system. He wanted her and only her, and she loved it.

"No," she whispered, wanting nothing more than to please him as much as he had pleased her.

Moving slowly to the middle of the bed, Catarena turned and dropped gracefully forward, presenting her body like a jewel before a king. A deep groan escaped from Mason's mouth, telling Catarena in a way no words would ever be able to that he loved what he saw. Her vagina wet and inviting, her ass engulfing a toy he had carefully picked out for her, Catarena was primed and ready for him.

The bed dipped as Mason eased onto it, positioning himself behind her. The wrapper of the condom slid down next to her leg as Catarena waited anxiously for him to make a move, any move, but he didn't. Looking over her shoulder, she peered at him and saw a look of pure lust on his face. Moving slowly, Mason reached out his hand to her.

"You look so beautiful," Mason said as he rubbed the round globes of her ass, moving his fingers to gently caress her crease and the plug still wedged inside her.

Mason took his time as he pushed the head of his cock into her wet entrance. Biting down onto her lip, Catarena instinctively braced herself for the pain of having two holes filled at once. She held her breath as Mason slid forward, seating himself into her depths. When he pushed in as far as he could go, Mason paused, staying still inside her, allowing her body to adjust to the thickness of both him and the plug.

"You feel so fucking good, baby," he murmured, flexing himself inside her. "So hot and juicy. Can you feel it? Feel what it's like to be filled completely?"

"God, yes," she moaned, as he slowly pulled out and pushed forward again. Moaning, Catarena dropped forward, laying her breasts flat on the bed, allowing for more lift to her hips. She felt unbelievably full. The plug lodged in her bore down a heavy weight in her womb, pushing down on Mason's cock as he pushed up into it.

Slow and steady, Mason gripped her hips as he plunged into her aching pussy. He began to build up his speed, working himself into her as he pulled her back against him firmly, causing his pelvis to slap against her ass. The vibrations were shaking the plug, forcing it to jar inside her, teasing and taunting her with stinging bites of pleasure.

"That's it, Kitten, that's it." Mason groaned as her pussy quivered around him. Arching up and crying out, Catarena shook with need as he drove into her persistently, increasing his speed to suit his strokes. It felt as if Mason were demanding more than her body—more like her soul.

The pleasure was immense, the need was undeniable, but still something was missing. Catarena clung to the bedsheets, digging into them with her nails, holding on with all her might as Mason powered into her from behind. She felt as if she could barely catch her breath with all sensations flowing through her at once. Pleasure and pain were colliding, burning her up from the inside.

"Move back onto me, Kitten," he gritted out roughly. Mason's fingers bit into the flesh of her side, dragging her back onto him. "Fuck yourself on my cock."

It was too much for her to bear. Catarena was so close yet still she couldn't come. Sobbing, she pushed back onto him begging with her body for more of his cock. "I can't... I can't..."

"Yes, you can," Mason growled, releasing her hip. "I know what you need, Kitten."

Catarena was stunned when she felt the first slap fall against her ass. It jarred her senses and the plug all at the same time, but when the second one came, she was more than ready—she was completely begging for it. The light smacks, the plug and the feel of Mason pumping into her were just what she needed. By the time the fourth slap landed on her tender ass, Catarena threw back her head and screamed her release, surrounding Mason's cock and the sheets with her juices.

"Yes, Kitten, yes." Mason grabbed the end of the plug and gave it a final twist, causing Catarena to lift up and shove back as hard as she could on his cock. Groaning, Mason cried out when he found his release mere seconds after Catarena's, pushing himself still farther into her, riding his orgasm out.

"Fuck, fuck, fuck," he muttered over and over again, as he pumped into her, finally slowing down as his need was met.

Releasing her grip, Catarena spread her fingers out, giving them a well-deserved break for holding her together for so long. She wasn't sure how she'd survived such pleasure but she had. She winced a bit when Mason tugged on the plug and let out a soft protest, groaning "no more" as she felt it slowly move out of her body.

Mason chuckled softly. "Don't worry, Kitten, we're all done."

"Thank God," she groaned as he eased out of her as well. Tired and exhausted, Catarena moved her legs from beneath her and dropped limply down onto her bed. Her body trembled from the strain of the pleasure and the pain, and all she wanted to do was sleep. She had heard of people passing out during sex, but she had never believed them—until now.

The bed moved as Mason rose, but Catarena was too tired to look to see where or what he was doing. Her room seemed a bit chillier, probably a result from the sweat coating her damp skin. Blindly she reached out for her comforter and groaned when she felt it move up her body. Mason sat down next to her head and pushed her damp hair away from her face.

"Are you all right, Kitten?" he asked with a slight hitch to his voice.

"No, I ache everywhere." Peeking one eye open, she looked up at him and smiled. "Isn't it cool."

Chuckling, Mason stroked her arm. "You won't think it's so cool tomorrow when you're too sore to sit down."

"Hey, who was the one playing with the plug?"

"Who was the one who wanted me to?"

"That's beside the point," she murmured, feeling a bit embarrassed at her wanton behavior. "But you're probably right. If you'll go start me a shower, I'll be your slave for life."

"Can I get it in writing?" he asked dryly, getting up.

Mason turned the water on and helped her into the shower. Stepping in behind her, he lovingly washed her entire body, stopping along the way to kiss and caress his favorite parts. Catarena for the most part just stood under the pounding water and allowed him to pamper her.

The steam filled the small bathroom, surrounding her with a cloudlike haven. Never before had Catarena felt so cherished, so loved, by someone. Unable to hold back the words which had been tumbling around in her mind, she slid her hands up to her hair, interlocking her fingers with Mason who was shampooing her, moved his soapy fingers down to her heart and leaned back against him. Softly, she murmured, "I love you." Half afraid to say it too loud in fear of his reaction—but to her surprise, Mason pulled her back into him roughly and replied, "I love you too."

Turning around in his tight embrace, Catarena looked up at him, moving her hands up to cup his face. "Say it again," she demanded, wanting to hear it again and again.

"I love you, Kitten."

Putting all of her love and desire into it, Catarena eased up to her tiptoes and attached her mouth to his, kissing him with everything she was made of. Their tongues played against one another as they exchanged not only words but joy. Easing away, Catarena closed her eyes and leaned against Mason's wet chest. It was more than she'd hoped for but all that she'd craved.

Mason rinsed off first and then stepped out of the shower to get a fresh towel for Catarena. He dried her off then wrapped her hair up with another, which she used to twist it until it was up off her shoulders.

Catarena followed Mason into the bedroom, slipped on her robe and handed him his boxers. "You need a drawer over here," she commented as she lathered her skin in vanilla-scented lotion.

"I have plenty of drawer space at my place. Room for me and you both," Mason countered.

Sighing, Catarena didn't want to get into this now. She knew it was a sore point with Mason but despite his dedication of love, she was still nervous. Change wasn't something she handled well, and the fact Mason wanted her to give up everything she knew and loved to be with him in his world scared her.

"Yes, you have drawer space, but do you have a neighbor who watches old Seventies porn movies really loud?" she joked, trying to ease the silence which had come over the room.

"Not that I'm aware of," Mason replied dryly.

"See, loud porn is something I need. I can't go to sleep without hearing 'bong chicka bong bong' every now and then."

"Right."

"Uh-huh. You think it's an excuse but it's true. I could be bribed though." Eyeing him, she smiled a wicked smile and added, "How against being cuffed are you again?"

"Don't even think about it."

Laughing, Catarena replied, "That's what I thought. I'm going to go get something to drink, you want anything?"

"No, I'm fine."

"Okay." Leaving her bedroom, Catarena paused by Bailey's room and peered in. She was still gone. How odd, she thought. Getting a glass of water, she returned to the room with a smile on her face, which immediately dropped when she faced a furious-looking Mason.

"What's wrong?" she asked, shutting the door behind her.

"Who the fuck is Master Paul," Mason demanded.

Catarena set her glass down. She was no longer smiling but she also wasn't acting the least bit guilty, making Mason madder than hell.

"I asked you who he is."

She put her hands on her hips then narrowed her eyes at him. "No, you didn't. You asked me who the *fuck* is he, which is completely different."

"Catarena," Mason couldn't help the anger and exasperation in his voice. The thought of her starting an online relationship with another man was enough to make him stark, raving mad.

"Good grief, Mason, he's just a man I've been emailing for research. He's a living, breathing Master who has studied and lived the lifestyle for many years."

Catarena moved past him, opening the door as she continued into the living room. Mason followed close behind, her printed email still clasped tightly in his hand.

"I don't give a shit who he is," Mason snarled. "I don't want you emailing him anymore."

He should have known his highhanded command wouldn't go over well with his Kitten. She stiffened up like a board then stalked over to where he was standing.

Gesturing wildly, she said, "We've been over this before. I won't be told what to do, especially when it comes to research and my writing. I don't get you, Mason. Why, when things are going so well, do you have to turn back into an asshole?"

Mason figured it was a rhetorical question, not one she expected him to answer. His eyes skimmed the content of the email for the second time. The man who called himself Master Paul went into detail about different types of BDSM rope tricks. He also talked in detail about giving a woman the right combination of pleasure and pain and what signs to look for while doing it. The section on spanking and the different implements a Master could use was also painstakingly written. What pissed Mason off most of all was that each and every answer was the result of a specific question asked by BlackCat—his Kitten!

"I told you I would help you with your research." Mason didn't want to admit it, his anger wouldn't let him see it, but the fact she'd turned elsewhere without saying a word to him was what was bothering him most of all.

"You have helped me, Mason," she said the words low as she moved closer to him. "But there are many aspects you're out of the loop on since you're not active in the lifestyle anymore. I just want to do the best I possibly can when it comes to my writing. I'll do whatever it takes."

Catarena put her hand out as if to touch his arm. Mason pulled away as if he'd been burned. She'd do whatever it took for her damned book. The words played over and over in his head.

"Whatever it takes, Kitten." The endearment no longer sounded loving. "Like fucking yourself on command in front of a webcam, Kitten?" he sneered the words. "Like going to a sleazy club and allowing strangers to grope you. But it's okay as long as it's in the name of research, right?"

Mason felt like scum when her beautiful face paled but it was done. The cruel words had already been said. There was no calling them back.

He waited for her to explode. Handling an irate Catarena Vaughan was bad enough but the quiet woman in front of him scared the hell out of him.

"You're a bastard, Mr. Broderick, but I assume you've been called worse." Her words were quiet, her voice low. The unshed tears making her eyes glitter tugged at his heart as no other woman's tears ever had. Had it only been moments ago they'd shared words of love? Mason idly wondered how things could get so royally screwed up in such a short amount of time.

"I want you to leave."

Damn, her words sounded final and there was no way Mason was going to settle for it. "I'm not leaving, Catarena, so you can just forget it."

"Then I will," she said as she turned and walked away from him, her shoulders square, her head held high. When she reached the door of her bedroom, she looked him right in the eye. "If I don't hear you leave within the next five minutes, I'll be calling the police and then my brothers. I'm not sure which would be worse, but if I were you, I wouldn't wait around to find out." With those words, the door snapped closed. Mason heard the snick of the lock even from where he stood in the living room.

When the lock sounded once again, Mason breathed a sign of relief, until his clothes came sailing toward him. "You might need these," was all she said before slamming the door once more.

"Son of a bitch!" he mumbled. Mason pulled his clothes on cursing a blue streak all the while. He was still angry with Catarena but he instinctively knew he'd gone about the whole thing the wrong way. Mason stalked up the hallway until he was facing her bedroom door. He banged on the door. "This isn't over, Kitten."

"Yes, Mason, it is. If you'd have asked, I'd have told you Master Paul lives halfway around the world with his consensual slave who also happens to be his wife. He is teaching me what I need to know to give my book the accuracy it was lacking, but you don't care about that. All you care about is keeping me under your thumb. I told you I can't live like that. I won't." Her voice was strong. Mason could hear the resolve. She meant exactly what she said.

"I can't be with someone who doesn't trust me, so just go away. I know what you think of me now, your parting shot made it clear."

"Trust?" he yelled through the door. "If you want to talk about trust then why don't we go over the reason you won't move in with me and what's wrong with the places I frequent? Hell, I almost had to twist your arm to get you to go out with me tonight." Mason was on a roll. He needed to get it all out in the open. "I might be able to understand you aren't ready to move in but you won't even stay the night at my place. How's that for trust, Kitten. Tell me that!"

God, he was tired of the fight already. He wanted nothing more than to pull her into his arms and hold her. Her next words blew his thoughts all to hell. "I'm done talking, now I'm picking up the phone."

Mason could hear the tears in her voice this time and was mentally kicking his own ass. *It's not over* was all he could think as he slammed out of her apartment.

That night was among the worst of his life. Mason had become so accustomed to having Catarena in his arms he felt lost. He could hear the husky whisper of her voice as she'd told him she loved him and the strength in his mirrored answer. By the time he drifted off to sleep, he was so mentally exhausted he didn't have much of a choice.

The following morning proved to be no better when he was late getting to the office only to learn his Kitten hadn't come in. When Mason called and only the recorded voice message on her machine answered, he wanted to kill.

Just before lunch, he heard voices outside his office door. His heart leapt in his throat thinking it might be Catarena. Maybe she had just been late, the same as he had. Mason launched himself from his chair, taking only a few, quick, long-legged strides to reach the door. He wretched it open to find Bailey delivering the mail to Mrs. Garner.

"Where's Catarena?" Mason asked before giving thought to how the growled question might be taken.

"You don't deserve to know." Her glare changed to a quick smile as she nodded goodbye to Mrs. Garner then stepped up to the elevator doors.

Mason couldn't help himself so after lunch he called down to the mailroom. He was told Miss Vaughan had finally shown and due to her tardiness and the lack of a phone call, she'd been written up for it.

The voice on the other end of the phone rubbed Mason the wrong way, giving him an uneasy feeling, but the happiness at knowing she'd finally shown up for work quickly took over. Mason knew it would be hard to do but he had to apologize.

His words wouldn't make everything better, they'd still have a whole lot of talking to do before things could return to normal—if it was even possible at this point. Mason was willing to do anything to have his Kitten back in his life.

The thought brought him up short. He was willing to do anything for Catarena because she mattered, she was important. It was the same sentiment she had used when speaking of her writing. For the first time since meeting her, he finally understood just how significant Catarena's writing was to her. Mason cursed himself again for being such an ass.

Once again seated behind his desk, Mason tried to concentrate on his work. He muddled his way through a few conference calls and even managed a meeting without seeming like a complete idiot, but that was as far as he got. If he didn't see his Kitten and get the chance to set things straight, he was going to go ballistic.

With that thought embedded firmly in his mind, he left his office and headed toward the elevators. This time he'd go to her. It was the least he could do after the way he'd treated her.

Chapter Fifteen

ജ

"Just dropped off the package to the evil one," Bailey commented, leaning against the sorting room's doorframe. "And if it's any consolation, he looked utterly miserable."

Continuing to sort the mail, Catarena refused to be swayed. "It probably was just gas or his normal scowl. They both resemble misery."

"Please, I know gas when I see it. Besides this one was different."

"How so?"

"Because it didn't have its usual grimace to it. He's hurting, girl."

Catarena looked up and smiled. She knew Bailey was just trying to make her feel better, but it wasn't really working. Instead of last night being one of the most romantic evenings of her life, it turned into one of the most miserable. Just when she had thought she was getting past Mason's overbearing ways, he would up and open his big mouth.

"It doesn't matter. He's never going to change." It had taken two boxes of tissues and the worst night of tossing and turning in her life for her to figure it out. Mason was just flat-out controlling—always had been, always will be.

"Well, now that you mentioned it, you're right. He never is. So what's your problem?"

Startled, Catarena turned around and faced her. "What do you mean 'what's my problem'? He went all caveman on me. Jumping to conclusion just because—"

"Just because he's mad crazy about you and he found out you were emailing some other guy."

She wasn't going to let Bailey simplify it like that. There was more to it. Like…like more. "So? He should have had enough trust in me to know it wasn't the case."

"And you should have had enough common sense to know if he found out any other way besides from your own mouth he was going to have a hissy fit. Get real, Cat, the man is crazy for you. Willing to do anything you want, and you won't even spend the night over at his house. Doesn't seem to me as if he's the only one with trust issues."

"Excuse me." Putting her hand on her hip, Catarena frowned. This wasn't the Bailey she was used to. Bailey was suppose to be her friend not evil Mason's. "Did you forget whose side you're on?"

Bailey rolled her eyes and walked all the way into the room. "I'm on your side, it's just this time your side isn't right, boo. Mason loves you, and I know you love him. You can't expect him to give and give when you won't either."

"Since when did you become a psychiatrist?" Catarena didn't want to admit it, but she knew Bailey was right about a lot of things. Things were just a lot easier when she could blame Mason for everything.

"When it came to you? Always." Taking her friend in her arms, Bailey gave Catarena a big hug before pulling back and looking her dead in the eyes. "I'm kicking you out of the apartment."

Catarena couldn't have been more surprised if Bailey had said she was running away with Stan and going to have his love child. "What?"

"I want you to get home and pack your stuff and hightail your rusty-dusty over to Mason's. I want a June wedding and a mess load of god-babies to play with." Letting her go, Bailey walked back to the door.

"Wait," Catarena called to her. "You just can't kick me out."

Bailey looked over and smiled. "Sure I can. I'm bigger, stronger and the apartment is in my name."

What the fuck? Catarena thought, watching her former best friend walk out the door. See, it never failed. Just when she thought things couldn't get any worse, she'd go and open her big mouth and prove herself wrong. She knew Bailey thought she was doing the right thing, but Catarena couldn't just show up at Mason's house and say, "Hi, honey, I'm home". They had things they needed to discuss. They had rules they needed to lay down. They had…well, hell, they were in love.

Turning back to her table, she shook her head and smiled. Only Bailey would do something so brash and call it helping. When she got home tonight she was going to—

A loud voice booming, "There you are", scared Catarena out of her thoughts. Looking over her shoulder, she gave a mental groan when she saw Stan standing in the doorway.

"Mr. Broderick called down here looking for you," Stan said, with amusement in his voice. "Didn't seem too happy to hear of the trouble you've started. Trouble in paradise already?"

"Just go away," Catarena muttered, refusing to give in to his bait.

"Ah, ah, ah, Ms. Vaughn. Looks like you might be losing your ace in the hole. I think you should start being a bit more friendly to the locals again, don't you?" Catarena jumped when she felt Stan run his fingers up her arm. She hadn't even heard him move.

Backing away from him, she rubbed her arm where he'd touched her, trying to erase his touch. "Don't touch me. Don't you ever touch me!"

Stan's face became blotched with rage. Turning, he walked to the door and Catarena gave out a sigh of relief because she thought he was leaving, but she was wrong. Shutting the door, Stan turned and walked toward her with an evil glimmer in his eyes. "I think you need to learn proper respect for authority."

Was he kidding? Did he really think she was afraid of him? "What I think is that you'd better open the door right now."

"I don't think so."

Looking at him, Catarena wondered if she'd ever really known who he was. Stan had always seemed a bit off, but not this off. "You do realize all I have to do is scream and the door will burst open and everyone will see what you're doing?"

"Why are you playing so hard to get? I bet Million Dollars Mason didn't have this hard of a time getting into your pants."

"You're not Mason." Catarena knew it wasn't right to egg him on, but she was tired of his bullying ways. Stan didn't scare her—he amused her—just another small-dick man trying to prove something to himself and everyone around him.

"But that's all it takes right? Flash a little green and bitches like you will spread faster than butter."

"Not only am I going to go to personnel and file a complaint, I'm going to a lawyer and sue your paisley tie-wearing ass for all your worth." Her brazen attitude shocked Stan who was probably expecting her to cower at his feet. "Open the door right now or you're going to regret it."

"Why don't you make me?" he replied cockily, not moving from in front of her.

Catarena moved to walk around him, but he grabbed her by the arm and pulled her back. "Not so bold when the big boss ain't covering your ass anymore."

Looking down at him with all the contempt and disgust she felt, Catarena said, "I'm just as bold, and for your information, we're still together, and when he hears about what you tried to do, firing is going to be the least of your worries." Snatching her arm away, she walked quickly to the door.

Catarena reached out, her fingers barely brushing the knob when Stan grabbed the back of her hair and pulled with all of his might, flinging her to the ground. Startled and upset, Catarena reached her hand up to touch the back of her head, wincing at the throbbing pain coming from her scalp. The weaselly bastard had put his hand on her. He wouldn't live to see the next day.

Stan loomed over her, smiling down at her from where he stood. Nudging her with his foot, he smiled as she scooted out of the way. "Scream for me, bitch."

"You first." Catarena moved quickly, aiming her foot back at his groin, kicking with all of her might. Thanks to numerous bouts of mock fighting with her brothers, her aim was dead-on.

Gripping his groin, Stan's eyes widened in shock and horror as he dropped to his knees, cupping his balls. Jumping up, Catarena watch the murderous rage come over his face as he released his hold on his privates and threw himself at her, knocking her back down to the floor.

"You stupid bitch..." he growled, pulling his fist back. Catarena countered by shoving her hands up as fast as she could and pushing with all her might, aiming for his nose. Letting out a bloodcurdling yell, Stan rolled off her, cupping his now bleeding nose.

His blood splattered across the front of her yellow shirt. For someone who had only just had her hair pulled, Catarena looked as if she had been attacked by a rabid dog. Looking over at Stan as she slowly stood back up, she guessed in a way she had. Something was wrong with him. No one acted that crazy just because of jealousy.

"I'm going to mill do bit," he muttered, muffling his words because of the hand covering his face. Catarena thought his muffled words sounded a lot like a threat to kill her, and that both pissed her off and scared her at the same time. She knew she could fight him until doomsday and he wasn't going to stop. He was twisted and obviously not in his right mind. Intent on getting help, Catarena turned to head for the door when he roared from behind her, on his feet again. Pulling the door open quickly, she ran right into Mason. He took one look at her blouse spattered in blood and at Stan who looked out of his mind and slammed the door behind him with murder in his eyes.

Anger so great he'd never felt anything even close to it had Mason bolting forward. The feel of bone crunching as his fist connected with the mailroom supervisor's face did nothing to diminish the height of his anger.

"Mason, no!"

The words sounded as if they were coming at him from a distance. The feel of Catarena's arms on him brought Mason out of the deep need to do bodily harm to Douglas. When he lowered his arm, his chest still heaving, Catarena moved in front of him.

She took his face in her hands and brought his mouth down for a short but sweet kiss before looking deep into his eyes. "I'm okay, really."

Mason narrowed his eyes, scrutinizing her face as if he could see what was inside her head. He had no choice but to listen to her softly spoken words.

"Look at him, Mason. Look at him. I took care of him. At least I tried."

The last of her breath quivered from her trembling lips and finally brought Mason completely back to the here and now. The first thing he noticed was how her soft hands were cold and shaking as they held his face. He turned to look at Douglas who was bent over double, cupping his balls with one hand while trying to staunch the flow of blood from his nose with the other.

"You did great, baby." The words rumbled from deep within his chest as he scooped his Kitten into his arms.

Mason took the few steps it would take to bring him to the door. He opened it, being careful not to jar Catarena. Now that his mind was working, all he could think to do was to get her to his office where he could check her over from head to toe and make sure she was all right.

A movement out of the corner of Mason's eye caught his attention. Without even turning he growled, "You so much as take a step and I'll break both of your fucking legs."

His ex-employee stopped where he was, rage mottled his face and twisted his features even more than Mason's fist had. "I've been working for you for years, I can't believe you're going to take the side of this cock-tease over me."

Mason took an intimidating step toward the man when he felt Catarena's hand on his arm. "He's not worth it, Mason." Her words were a mere whisper yanking Mason out of the red haze of anger that had threatened to overtake him. He pulled Catarena close to him then reached for the door.

Finally, in the hall just beyond the room where the attack had taken place, Mason bellowed into the intercom for a security guard. It was several seconds before the uniformed man came barreling around the corner. Mason didn't wait before barking out orders.

"Ms. Vaughan was attacked. You'll find the culprit in that room," he said, nodding to the door just up the hall from them. "Call the police then take care of the trash until they arrive."

"Yes, sir," the man answered pulling a handheld radio from a uniform pocket. Mason heard voices muffled with the radio's static as the elevator doors closed.

It was the longest walk of his life. Catarena said nothing, just burrowed her face against his chest. She wasn't crying but Mason could feel the trembling of her body. He prayed the entire way to his office she wasn't hurt.

"I'm okay, Mason. Just a bit shaken up is all." Her words sounded sincere but Mason had a mind to check for himself.

"You could put me down." She tried again, even giving a good wiggle this time around.

"Stay still, Kitten, and you won't be going anywhere until I check you out myself. By then the police ought to be here so we can file charges." Mason's worry soared to new levels when she didn't argue or retort with a sassy comeback.

Mason carried Catarena through the now opened elevator door and into his office. Mrs. Garner sprang to her feet.

"Oh, dear! Is she all right?"

Mason wasn't sure exactly how to answer. "Some water, please," he said instead.

Mrs. Garner asked no more questions. Instead, she headed to the executive washroom to do as he asked.

Mason entered his office then sat Catarena gently on the couch. He didn't realize how bad his own hands were shaking until he started running them methodically over her body.

Her blouse was splattered with blood. The sight made him want to go back downstairs and knock the hell out of Douglas all over again.

"I'm fine, Mason."

"I don't know, baby. Maybe we should call for an ambulance." He needed to hear she was going to be fine.

"Mason, look at me."

Mason finished running his hands over her body, checking quickly for any broken bones or cuts then he did as she asked. Color bloomed in her cheeks and she was no longer shaking as much.

"He didn't get the chance to hurt me bad, Mason. I promise you. He pulled my hair and talked a lot of shit, but that's it."

Mason looked down at her blouse. The sight made him ill. To think something so horrendous could happen in his building was hard to handle.

"This is his blood, Mason, none of it's mine. Other than kicking him in the nuts, I think I broke his nose, but nothing happened to me."

Mason did everything possible to hide his anger. The fact Douglas had had the audacity to lay his hands on his woman made Mason want to rip the man to pieces. It seemed as if hours had passed when the police finally left with report in hand. Douglas had long since been taken away in cuffs.

When Bailey showed up to coddle her best friend, Mason thought he might never have his Kitten to himself again. He waited as long as his patience would allow before letting Bailey know they would be leaving.

"Time to go, Kitten. Say goodbye to Bailey." They both stared at him as if he'd lost his mind but Mason had a lot he needed to say and it wouldn't wait long because of the overwhelming need to get his Kitten naked so he could hold her close — flesh to flesh.

Mason was surprised when instead of arguing, Bailey winked and gave him a thumbs-up. Mason returned the gesture with a wink of his own just before he scooped Catarena back into his arms and strode for the door. Bailey opened it for him, shocking him once again.

The ride to his house was quiet, even a bit tense. When they reached his place, Mason gave in to Catarena's pleas to walk, although what he really wanted was to hold her tight and never let her go.

Inside his house, Mason led them up the hall to his room where he settled Catarena into one of the overstuffed chairs nestled into the corner. Instead of taking the other chair for himself, Mason sat on the footstool directly in front of her, facing her.

"I told you I was okay," she said sounding a bit defensive. "You're going to make me mad if you don't believe me, and I don't want to be mad anymore. I missed you when we were mad."

It was hard for Mason to swallow much less talk — his throat was thick with emotion. "I don't want to be mad anymore either, baby. As a matter of fact, what I want is your forgiveness. I never meant to hurt you the way I did. I didn't understand how important your writing is to you, but now I do."

Her eyes were bright with unshed tears as he reached out for her hands. Squeezing his back, she said, "You do?"

"I do, Kitten. I didn't at first, but I do realize it now. I just want you to be happy…"

Mason had to stop and take a deep breath. The intoxicating anger he'd felt still lingered just beneath the surface. "When I walked into the mailroom and saw what Douglas was doing, I wanted to kill him. A part of me still does. God, baby, I don't ever want to feel like that again. Tell me we can work this out. Tell me you'll be mine forever."

His voice was insistent but he could no longer hold back what was inside. When she looked at him—a sheepish smile on her face—Mason thought he'd died and gone to heaven.

"It won't be easy for either of us, but I'm game if you are."

Mason leaned in and captured her mouth in a searing kiss. Backing off, he said, "I'm game, Kitten."

Pulling her to her feet, Mason slowly began removing her soiled blouse. Catarena's voice was hesitant at first, causing his fingers to still.

"I don't know about fitting in with your friends and the fancy places you go. Heck, I'm afraid to touch anything here for fear it'll break. I just wanted you to know it didn't have anything to do with not trusting you."

Mason breathed a sigh of relief then chuckled. "That's what has you so worried?"

"Don't you laugh at me, Mason Broderick!"

Mason chuckled again as he finished undressing Catarena and then himself. When they were both nude, Mason led her to the shower where he washed away any remnants of her ordeal, making sure to caress every curve and linger over every valley.

After drying them both off, Mason led his Kitten to the bed where he snuggled up close behind her, loving the feel of her smooth, supple body nestled against his.

"I'll tell you what, baby. You can change this place however you like because from today on, it's your home just as much as it's mine. As for my friends, you've already met the one who counts the most. Now stop sweating the small stuff and start worrying about how you're going to keep me in line."

His Kitten giggled then wiggled her way around until she was face to face with him. Her wicked blue eyes were full of mischief as she said, "I'm sure I'll think of something," just before she disappeared beneath the blankets.

Mason sucked in a sharp breath at the feel of Catarena's mouth on the sensitive head of his partially aroused shaft. He smiled then mumbled to no one in particular, "I bet you will, Kitten. I bet you will."

Epilogue

ℛ

The past few weeks had proven to be very interesting. Catarena's excitement about her writing spilled over to Mason, exciting him as well. He was even becoming used to the fact she emailed other men and asked them sex questions. Hell, half the time he was as interested in the answers as she was.

With the long day's work finally over, Mason was passing time on the computer waiting for Catarena to arrive. He'd just finished putting into motion what he hoped would be one hell of a surprise for his Kitten. The champagne was chilling as was the light meal he'd had catered.

The wonderfully scented candles Catarena seemed to prefer surrounded the deep tub taking up one side of the master bathroom. Mason wanted so much for things to turn out perfectly. Tonight would hopefully mark the beginning of a new life for the both of them. A new life where his Kitten agreed to become Mrs. Catarena Broderick.

Mason was jolted when the computer sounded and his Instant Messenger box popped up.

BlackCat: Hi.

The single word brought a smile to his face.

Maverick: Hi, Kitten, why aren't you on your way over?

There was a pause before the next message flashed before his eyes.

BlackCat: I had a few notes to print out from Master Paul before clearing out the hard drive for Bailey. You're going to love these ones.

It was such an incredible feeling to love and be loved that Mason had a hard time explaining it, even to himself. Throughout everything, Catarena hadn't asked even one more time about his obsession with control.

Mason figured it was because she knew it was something he was working on but tonight of all nights, he felt the need to show her he was doing more than just working on it. And although he would never be the type to give it all up, Mason was more than ready to experiment.

Maverick: Finish up as early as you can, baby.

BlackCat: And why is that?

Maverick: Because I have a surprise for you.

Mason maneuvered the mouse so he could start his webcam and sent a message for Catarena to do the same. It took a couple of seconds but soon Catarena's face and upper body could be seen in a little box on his computer's screen. The sight of the silver choker once again circling the delicate line of her neck had Mason's cock standing at attention.

BlackCat: So what's my surprise?

Catarena smiled at him, her head cocked to the side. Mason couldn't help but tease a bit.

Maverick: Always so impatient, Kitten.

BlackCat: Are you saying you aren't even going to give me a hint?

Mason could imagine the exasperation in her voice and it was almost as amusing as the way her bottom lip jaunted out in a little pout.

Maverick: Nope, not at all what I'm saying.

BlackCat: Then spill it, Mason. You're driving me crazy.

Maverick: Are you going to hurry?

Mason could clearly see his Kitten's face. She was irritated, her brows furrowed as she pondered the question.

BlackCat: Anything, just tell me already!

Mason didn't say a word. Instead, he dangled Catarena's shiny silver cuffs from his finger.

BlackCat: Are you serious? Don't mess with me, Mason.

Maverick: I'm not messing, Kitten. I love you and I trust you, but this is only part of the surprise, you'll get the rest when you get home.

BlackCat: I'm outta here.

Mason burst out laughing as he saw Catarena bolt from her chair. He rose from his seat and poured himself a glass of whiskey, contemplating what might happen when his Kitten made it home. After several minutes, he sat back down at the desk and was just about to log off when Bailey sat in the exact same spot Catarena had recently vacated.

BlackCat: I don't know what you said to her but she almost mowed me over getting out the door.

Mason wasn't about to tell Bailey he'd told Catarena she could cuff him to the bed and have her wicked way with him. Hell, half the office building would know it before morning.

Maverick: I told her I had a surprise for her. Shouldn't you be out on a date or something?

BlackCat: I am.

Mason watched as she turned to look over her shoulder. Behind her, standing in the bedroom door was a person. Mason could only see the lower half of the person's body but from the clothing, it appeared to be a man.

BlackCat: It was really nice of Cat to leave me her computer, but I don't have much time to play these days…on the computer that is.

The words popped onto Mason's screen even as he watched the man move closer.

BlackCat: Time for me to go.

Bailey waved goodbye to the webcam and Mason. Before she logged off though, Mason got a very clear shot of a hand resting on Bailey's shoulder. The hand bore a ring he was more than familiar with. It was familiar because it was the same exact ring his best friend Sebastian wore.

Why an electronic book?

We live in the Information Age—an exciting time in the history of human civilization in which technology rules supreme and continues to progress in leaps and bounds every minute of every hour of every day. For a multitude of reasons, more and more avid literary fans are opting to purchase e-books instead of paperbacks. The question to those not yet initiated to the world of electronic reading is simply: *why?*

1. *Price.* An electronic title at Ellora's Cave Publishing and Cerridwen Press runs anywhere from 40-75% less than the cover price of the <u>exact same title</u> in paperback format. Why? Cold mathematics. It is less expensive to publish an e-book than it is to publish a paperback, so the savings are passed along to the consumer.

2. *Space.* Running out of room to house your paperback books? That is one worry you will never have with electronic novels. For a low one-time cost, you can purchase a handheld computer designed specifically for e-reading purposes. Many e-readers are larger than the average handheld, giving you plenty of screen room. Better yet, hundreds of titles can be stored within your new library—a single microchip. (Please note that Ellora's Cave and Cerridwen Press does not endorse any specific brands. You can check our website at www.ellorascave.com or

www.cerridwenpress.com for customer recommendations we make available to new consumers.)

3. *Mobility.* Because your new library now consists of only a microchip, your entire cache of books can be taken with you wherever you go.

4. *Personal preferences are accounted for.* Are the words you are currently reading too small? Too large? Too...**ANNOYING**? Paperback books cannot be modified according to personal preferences, but e-books can.

5. *Instant gratification.* Is it the middle of the night and all the bookstores are closed? Are you tired of waiting days—sometimes weeks—for online and offline bookstores to ship the novels you bought? Ellora's Cave Publishing sells instantaneous downloads 24 hours a day, 7 days a week, 365 days a year. Our e-book delivery system is 100% automated, meaning your order is filled as soon as you pay for it.

Those are a few of the top reasons why electronic novels are displacing paperbacks for many an avid reader. As always, Ellora's Cave and Cerridwen Press welcomes your questions and comments. We invite you to email us at service@ellorascave.com, service@cerridwenpress.com or write to us directly at: 1056 Home Ave. Akron OH 44310-3502.

THE
⚥ ELLORA'S CAVE ⚥
LIBRARY

Stay up to date with Ellora's Cave Titles in
Print with our Quarterly Catalog.

TO RECIEVE A CATALOG,
SEND AN EMAIL WITH YOUR NAME
AND MAILING ADDRESS TO:

CATALOG@ELLORASCAVE.COM
OR SEND A LETTER OR POSTCARD
WITH YOUR MAILING ADDRESS TO:

CATALOG REQUEST
C/O ELLORA'S CAVE PUBLISHING, INC.
1056 HOME AVENUE
AKRON, OHIO 44310-3502

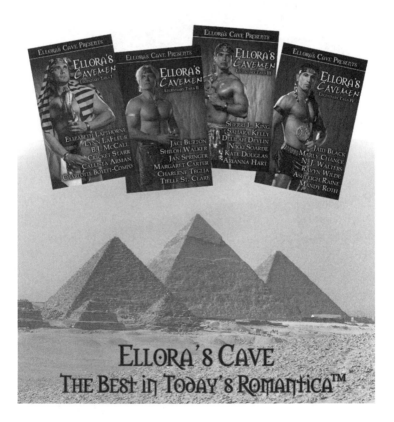

ELLORA'S CAVEMEN

TALES FROM THE TEMPLE

Try an e-book for your immediate
reading pleasure or order these titles in print from

www.EllorasCave.com

ELLORA'S CAVE
THE BEST IN TODAY'S ROMANTICA™

Make each day more *EXCITING* With our

Ellora's
Cavemen
Calendar

Monday

Tuesday

Wednr

Sunday

 www.EllorasCave.com

erridwen, the Celtic Goddess of wisdom, was the muse who brought inspiration to storytellers and those in the creative arts. Cerridwen Press encompasses the best and most innovative stories in all genres of today's fiction. Visit our site and discover the newest titles by talented authors who still get inspired - much like the ancient storytellers did, once upon a time.